What Matters: Writing 1968-70

DAPHNE MARLATT
What Matters: Writing 1968-70

The Coach House Press · Toronto

Published with the assistance of the Canada Council
and the Ontario Arts Council.

ISBN 0-88910-161-2

for Kit

Of the matter

Material, what matters. Indeed what (grave) matters & does it matter to anyone but myself? There are passages we all make, & which i take as evidence of a common condition, being alive at this point in time, or as alive as consciousness & an effort to fight off the closed terms of our culture will allow. What follows is evidence of one passage, or one story, or one version of a common story. To begin with,

In 1968, my husband Al & i were living in the Napa Valley in California, each of us having finished several years of graduate work at Indiana University & supposedly heading for home, Vancouver, BC. He was finishing the last requirement for his doctorate in clinical psychology – an internship at Napa State Hospital. I was doing a little teaching & some writing. In the fall of that year a job came through for him from the Psychiatry & Psychology Departments at UBC. We returned home as we always knew or imagined we would. Our child was born there but the job didn't fit & by the fall of 1969 we were back in the States, in Wisconsin, where he was teaching in the Psychology Department at UW. I was writing about Vancouver, watching our son grow, & wondering what i was doing on a tobacco farm in the American Midwest. By the end of 1970 i had come home to Vancouver with Kit for good (as it has since been).

So the writing in this book resonates, much of it, with what is known as alienation, living as i was in another country, & feeling estranged (which of us was the stranger in that struggle for the real) in my marriage & among friends. I was moved by the issues raised, & raging around us, by members of my generation – the Vietnam war, freedom of speech, equal rights, environmental ravages. But i didn't feel able to join the struggle, partly because grounds for it in the States seemed not to be my grounds, & living away from homeground i was ignorant of the struggle there. What *was* my ground? At issue, on a large scale, was a coming to own up to (take on) my place in a world i was part of & already compromised in. & this in & through those other turbulences of loving & 'losing' love (where did it go?), of first mothering, & of finding a voice to articulate any of it.

Articulate, join, fit the parts together, connect. Since adolescence i'd kept a sporadic journal which was not only an account of (trying to account for) my experience, but a workbook & a confessional. During these two years it rarely described my feelings & the more confused i felt the more desperately the journal tried to 'make sense.' Making sense became the work, generated by the fear that if i could not make sense of what was happening, then my life was indeed senseless & immaterial.

Yet at the same time i was writing poems, both short- & long-line, composing out of a poetic that taught me language, its 'drift,' could ground my experience in the turn of a line as tense, as double-edged, as being felt. In the oscillation of a pun, or a rhyming return, i sensed a narrative that wasn't only mine, though i participated in its telling & was thereby told. Caught up in it, connected, in the body of language where we also live.

What matters? what is the matter? or *what is the matter with you?* In the dialect i grew up speaking the latter question always implied that you were missing something, meaning 'not all there.' It took me a while to junk the last two words & arrive at the necessity of asking the first. & so to be present, to a place i could take on as home (with the response-abilities that implies), in a language i share with others — engaged, as definitive, & as quick, as the bodies we touch each other in. Of such matters, a celebration: that we are here, together, at all.

daphne marlatt
Vancouver 8/80

Contents

In the beginning was not the word. In the beginning is the hearing.

MARY DALY

If you don't understand the story you'd better tell it.

GEORGE BOWERING

California

let

your cock mine
a dark
light ahead

seek that
collapse of wall we
sometimes give in

will
what doorway's spent

     that lock

emptiness wears
lockt tight in it
self lockt

         hands
         will work

whose invention is
a door again

unlockt, opens on
some shared dark
carbide / car
nified

     Light —

what the cock knows
beyond crowing, spent

within

woke to sun's
white
        abstract of waking
warms with fullness the
fullers' sleave
curtains

where white lives
thickens, a

screen in which
i see you only
mindwise
cut on the bias o
    bleak to
    texture

beyond which limbs
the walnut glints

    bare now
unclothed fully

        sun

sun within arms'
reach

bugs in the heart

for Karen, 2 years old

moth, it
flies, this
fly-by-night

hurts no one

ii

night crawlers or
dew worms do
not rise at dawn

when the rains come down

night, they rise to
see what? flooded out &
drown

iii

daddy
long legs long
on white walls for
ground on which to
come down

wings mean
goals they never
reach, outreaching
legs, six, seize

no kids, never
anything but
space

iv

a slug
in a bed
no one covers

a kiss
no one ever
attempts it, a hug

is the best
earth can give

white gate

bare light
yellows unseen
back of hills
frogs harp

on ceremony, birthday
eyes secure
the avenue await
urbane grand
mother, father with

smiles, what
ever they
might bring

a gate / a light
wind night
settles

acacia (war

time's spine
sensitive to touch

woke to thru
window of yellow
while stood up

a look? a cup

leans deep into
today's well
being we drink from

whose right?

         hands a
cloud round me that
we stands for *i*
lies
    root in me
a radical whose tip
wears deeper
in re
    sistance

soakt & separate
blood strung
eyes we turn to
barely
    touch

'How can one of another show'

for D.

The supposed orginals were incarnate in all there is was
to have been ... a lawful movement. That the moment they
were, are 4, figures under a palace of fine arts etched
against moon illumined space or ground, whatever night was,
space took on their relations, seeking the central arch
over by & above the deepest (eye impenetrable) density of
pond.

There were swans, drift into eyeshot from trees.
& they were totally in fact white. Of cutouts one believed in
a particular something behind, a light say the depth of water
split to let out. She said *swans,* no they can't be are they?

While the gelatinous mass of the eyes, everything else granulate,
a texture of cement, & fingers in touch with it as eyes too
had been, duped into thinking the figure marble or alabaster,
whatever margins/maidens of that day wore as birdlands in the
grass. So the separate granules of i's wandered below a frieze
of figures out of reach had once too been before embalmed beyond
any instinctual relations, except these 2, a little gritty to
the sense of context:

there were cars outside, they had arrived
in his. The air was thick (wings) with betrayal, the barracks
life he said, a repetition of that golden round might well have
led them into a sense of their merry/

goes still finally here.
If there were guns they never heard them, but there could have been.
Silencers. No one dropt dead a question for shylocks as flesh
charged with colorless liquid froze on instant contact with

the outside.

These 2, their context out of hand that time translates
moving like leaves to show a passage from tree to tree. Acanthus.
They held.

& as to measure, he did, the equivalent of double
steps at a time they were that deep? Her eyes from below couldn't
quite make out except that he was careful with his feet, Said?
something no longer memorable it was so compounded with his stepping
flat against stone, that some young girl with garlands *would* at the
edge of accident come with various remedies & eyes wide open ...
her? She drew a blank. (the guns again, from several crannies.)

What was to be said? his words, erased off the faces of reconstructed
maidens, premeditated, or as a forecast of rain? She waited,
stiffer & stiffer. You know these arches are hollow? he offered,
a corner turned on their vista of lake. & she knew it was
over but just for the sake of it, yes? I've seen lights inside, a
table & chairs, a life. Oh where but *then*

the flutter clap & slash
of birds hit water, rocks or roots out from under the trees where she
was a bright sound. Ran, to look where the birds were, not, saw,

the only surface of water 4 peopled their interplay had, as it were,
gone.

perceive (apprehend, seize) what exists:

the bodies of words: their physical reality (sound)
their meanings ⎰ history & derivatives
⎱ association, ways of linking

'form is never more than an extension of content'
(comes) out of the tension of content — nothing exists without form, the
importance here is on the bodily insistence, the knitting of potential &
actual — a thought is an act: moves all of itself (out of desire towards
completion) & the desire is only completed when the thought stands/ in (no
other) words, at rest

poetics then consists of attention to extension (implication unfolded) —
no more the notion of filling up a form — but the *act*, out in the open

care with words means/words mean, with their interactions

May 26/68

on way down to get newspaper this morning thought I have not addressed
myself to purpose yet: of my life, how reflect it in the writing — ?

to be present, here, in this place: to find my ground. something more than pacing up & down the rows of Di Rosa's vineyard each morning. nowhere to walk in the country that is not marked off by some fence or row. the present we walk marked out for us: Al's internship & then his job (where?), my thesis & then my M.A. — for what? a teaching job somewhere (& do I know any *more?*)

reading the *Berkeley Barb* & thinking of having a child, of "bringing it into this world" — as if we were all equally present in it, all in the foreground. whose world? just procreating not enough, I want to make the world a securer place for him/her. any sort of political ideas are lacking from my work — to do with a lack of conviction that I also exist here, among?

May 28/68

today twice that welling up of the past in the present — stopping to let Al off today at 1:00, under those trees momentarily in the turnabout, a deep smell of earth brought back Spain to me — hot day, wind off highway, & then suddenly this *lush* earth smell.

then driving down Old Sonoma Road, a long triplex facing east, 2 Mexican boys at the balcony, children shouting — again that quick sense of my past alive in others' present —

realized what pushed me to writing was these intuitions of the other: inspiration I've since called it, interweaving of my life & a life outside me, as if I could see myself as an object within a more total relationship — something I don't know how to reach in paint or music but perhaps in words: the way they link up carrying their history

Niedecker:

"Nobody   nothing
   ever gave me
      greater thing

   than time
      unless light
         and silence"

pregnancy would be time made matter in me

                                        August 3/68

Ray Charles on radio wailing out: "you know there's something wrong,
baby" — *tired* of pushing it. last night's scene, thoughts of leaving SF,
making it on my own — not to do with Al so much I realize today as with the
writing, with me. I'm not completely here. writing on the borders, that
project, tends to get off center — not writing out of self but only out of head.
tired of my complicated prose style.

reading Dorn's *Rites of Passage* no doubt had its effect. but I'm not Dorn,
don't have that experience which necessitates the literal quality of his work,
as against real circumstances of poverty, illness, death. a hard edge against
the hard edge of life (a way of life anyhow — to make it/ cut it, out of U.S.
20th century life.)

mine's against a more abstract danger — mental survival, if you will — the
fear that things are not what they seem.

but what do I 'know'? not as knowledge but as experience, that is where the
writing starts. this year rather withdrawn. only realities are living with Al,

teaching, living on a ranch we don't have much to do with, outside of a town we don't have much to do with, in a country that is not ours. Dorn must have been writing every day to remember / record all those concrete details. to make headway with even the absence of certain things.

August 5/68

Merleau-Ponty speaks of perception as synthesis of form & matter (as one grasps the *unseen* side of an object one sees) & not as intellectual act ("possible", or "necessary" (because e.g. geometry teaches us that a rectangle has 4 sides) — perception grasps it as 'real': "the infinite sum of an indefinite series of perspectival views in each of which the object is given but in none of which is it given exhaustively" — cubism!

M-P also says: "the perceived thing ... exists only in so far as someone can perceive it. I cannot even for an instant imagine an object in itself." & then goes on "as Berkeley said, if I attempt to imagine some place in the world which has never been seen, the very fact that I imagine it makes me present at that place."

August 7/68

Mokelumne Hill Communique — communication itself the area to explore. striving for a realism there is more absorbing than in the novel where effectuality of communication is already assumed. effect of phenomenological reading: to catch the web of experience itself, not as thought (pursuit of an idea) which tends to shortcut sensory input, but the interplay of sensory being-in-a-place & thoughts about (connections with memory or surmise).

in contemporary American novel, perception, its primacy, has been over-lookt in favour of the ideational.

Sense of the other: approaching the Stein sense of portrait: in situ, what comes up in my consciousness of what we share, that 'place' in which we relate, fictionally at that time. levels of reality: brackets (parentheses).

Friday, August 23/68

today learned I am pregnant.

August 30/68

waiting for movers to come: last morning in the house: quiet, sunshine, birds talking. dreamt this morning I had to substitute again, this time in elementary school. the problem: trying to get information from uncoopera-tive kids ("who's away") — me the supposed authority figure not ever in the know — bad feeling from bad system.

thought I should write down my feelings about being pregnant & immedi-ately though that's more 'personal' than what else is in here. & then thought, why make that split? everything is personal, expresses a point of view. get into the unexpressed, press it out onto the page. feel that probably most of my thoughts re being pregnant are just like other women's: means I haven't really made it part of deepest consciousness yet, related it to deepest parts of my life — & that's due to fear at this stage of miscarrying. re/press/d.

difficult to think ahead as far as next spring, to the actual birth — in Vancou-ver — that seems right.

Time out
>   *for Susie*

Light must be assumed behind cloud faces — subsumed,
into the cold & damp there that is undergrowth, under
heaviness of trees moss flourishes wet, strings,
hair roots in.

>   Mossy? No, We had no name
either of us could think of then. Car parked in
shadow, cool after (wine, eyes in, sun). The
two men by the river, characteristic, one on
the embankment standing, other ranging into the
undergrowth. for small things, found things,
event,

>   Outcome, was it, slime? Hardly.
Reeds in the water, my eye entangled there while she
was talking. Topknots, hairy as grimes submerged in
ageless chimney pots (& we haven't screwed for, well)
more scary underwater than on fire.

>   Walking, I want
to walk, come down the bank (her stockinged feet in their
shoes). She speaks of an irritation membrane is
unaccustomed to. Needs air.

>   Not parasitic? No,
white. Fungi, sprung up in the silence of night.
She said, it's the idea that sickens me, as if,
it rots.
>   Or is it, alternative to sun, as cool here,
sunless rock wall moss & small things cling to. Even
the air is fetid, & the grass, drowned. Long

strings of it, in the water willowing back, under
the wall he stands on, with pipe. To stoke it, light it,
smoke.

Her husband walks further off, determined, in
no apparent direction into, bush. More simply
occupied by his attention.

Not that she lives off
her decay (air is what is needed) only, growth feeds on
the idea. A yeast, vegetate of its own seasonal
dilapidation.

So, in the dampness of unsunned wall we are
standing in, air, oozes slowly out of our mouths
... unheard. The water runs. My man smokes. An acridity,
an ash, a wild wandering aromatic that is gone now.
While he waits, awaits us, outwaits me in time.

Our friend is climbing back down, having found whatever
it was he put, directly, into her hand.

Mokelumne Hill

Of orange trees (angelica?) see green: as what the eye needs
morning when oil glazes skin. heat. (of the day's not to be
yet) this freshness, freshet, water, lifting the glass to lips,
comes on a sweet taste

                            after sour? Night. Night's mouth
sour − grapes at not being able to ... Repeat: they had got up
first, & bright. Our entrance from the hall must (from the
dark) have struck them as blind, day begun some hours already.
We see them small with table between, engaged in some kind of
close ... 'out on the verandah' ... morning. hits the face.
Or did he see them close? or even notice. Our choosing of
seats conservative (stumble): each woman between 2 men or
the reverse. Corners. Each to his own, her place.

                                 Faces white
with day raise distance (blank wall ahead,· is the form of a
question): A turning towards me (not) could watch trees past
D's head to building edge; C opposite has that surge in full
view; D also turning to ... a green eye juggles with

                               heat, skin
exposed his glance made no comment on: heat's small sweat
beads over forehead, upper lip. Of orange angelica (preserve
some sweetness) see green water we last swam in, A & me, in
silence, shine. 2 women below with kids undress, voices rise
(splash) nonsensical (what to do, do, not how) their children
calling, see me see me ...
                      to preserve (angelica) moment
of falling. All children wish to see themselves, to be seen ...

as 'up some hours already' (what have *you* done with your dawn?)
can be clarity at this hour, here only white, siding behind C's
head (or tipsy leaning?) 4 geometric on 4 legs rickety each on
flooring (at the mouth of a minehead

on pickaxes, they stand
some a little drunk their grins or tipsy leaning, lean over,
falling ... she. was stung by insult or. bore him heavily to
the point. in the photograph small, stands solemnly contained,
one man's arm slung easily round her neck, restraining ...

Yesterday dusty as what lies in the town museum after (night's
excitement). Little boots. Even axes look small. Or a revolver
fits in the palm almost miniature.
Surely it's the aftertaste
gone sour that wakes us.

So, 'climbed the hill looking for coffee. no place open' even
(sounds of the street: a bell) dog only solitary (tolls, heat
takes its toll) a morning kitchen help might sleep. angelus.
Some inevitable pacing of the day here (their plates of ham
look good)

slam: screen door air wisp hair, tired face, or
tired of sundays' sameness: ham coffee juice eggs.

had said
'any chance of coffee?' oh past her he recognized someplace
her leisurely walk. Banters, redhead? No, the one with the
tight ass ... scene from somewhere: that quiet glimpse of
someone's kitchen, still-hung pots depend, her flesh, its
working. Hadn't even noticed. Does A?

She says even before
that (evening, she had gone to bed first, 3 of us sitting in
chairs under the orange tree, 2 of us close) sun woke him,
or anyway never sleeps in, read, every page of the sunday
paper. Needs patent (walls between) all that activity light
thru newsprint ...

only woman hanged, it said, in this
part of the country. no angel yet ... she had her reasons.

Look, mama, look. Mama! (breakfast comes. her hand. blue
plates of ham grease won't jell on.) Look at me. I'm looking
No, *look* at me. (coffee cuts. the strawberry taste of jam good
with ham.)

D now on his 4th or 5th cup, wiping drops from
moustache, hears what (eyes down) she comments: thinks the whole
town should wake when he does (all that silence out there),
don't you, love? Unanswered. Mouth makes its gesture rue
some bitter pip (oldtime. old town. this town a movie set
we sit in, picturing ourselves.

I'd said, Yellow — the after
noon haze enthusiasm plays, for the image, A, will you take a
picture of the street? (climb thru window to verandah's edge)?
in view of the drop, grange or masonic hall's impossible stone
furthering windows, ways in ... He said take it from the street.

As from the street, *when*'re you coming to bed?

so need infects
the dream breath swells (unripe oranges last night slit by his
knife, green, hardly sections yet, or sectioned like some minute
flower pattern, unflesht as yet)

'The stink of your mouth at
breakfast'... a deep slap? If it hurts she only smiles.
Coffee
increases sweat, or secretes violence. Her hand level as any
man's to shoot him down.

Saloon set last night in theatrical
light of window piece, by piece, 1895, no not a date he said —
a number men remember. O the tiffany there you would not believe,
liqueurs, preserved sweets, swell tits theirs fingers unruffle,
largesse or, pianissimo! to raise us. They laugh together ...

One. shot in the dark. Will she see us when she comes down?
Double shot mid rows of bottles oh her small face appear, collar
up, out to sea, gravity of unmoved clang of the bar (boys)
nightlight ...

A's voice makes furred toward her. presence
at the table cuts. Not pathos, pathetica, heart-shape face.
Something dates her ... angelique? as of liqueur that was popular
then, speaking of men, midway between the angels &. it is that
slight tension walk she does, a line to maintain herself against
any falling for.

Or jumping-off place: they are into machines
that play violin & piano combined. they are into bottles &
gaslight & little boots ... I said how old do you think that
trunk is? which sits a yard or so behind me in this bar in
which ...

A's voice light with the last 5 minutes, the 'last'
double, the 'last' cut in a medley that lights & colours his
passing, coins changed, whirr of memory searches for, toward,
continues on past ...

I get up alone — was the trunk inviting hands, eyes? Whose lid
lifts heavy & round to imitate a chest (bust) must of paper
space to lie in, hide in, pack it all in — like them, no date
anonymous. D: a good idea. means, you've stepped outside the
set. stopped.

              Walls to remember, walls to project desire,
not even newsprint casts some light on — an abandoned piece
of luggage. abandoned wants, set in the museum after. She
at least, she acted on them.

Drain the last bit of orange from the glass: tipt up, throat
exposed to morning throbs, continuous life-line of want. & tho
the verandah slopes we sit on, into that space heat poses ...
orange tree vertical, its relief of green ...

                        Will that be
all now? (last drop) Who so stands, pencil poised, waiting
for the smallest nod to add us up, slap by A's plate ('thank
you' upside down), no smile even, to collect the plates.

Unripe oranges & a morning walk. What I know of him. Was last
night only audible scene. Hurried steps outside shutters 2
feet away. Heels. click click. angry. click. or hurried
(don't know what to think) ... Oh come on. (firmer footsteps
after) Don't you touch me! Let's go / Let go! (off the deep
end) & his 'wait' urgent now: was she going to jump?

                           Silence
prior to, as silence maintained in the museum after, space
for wants to contract in. So we move into the must of hall
in single file mount the stairs. Windows open, shutters open,
cool from the as yet unsunned street. unphotographed. & this
was ours.

To A: you missed the balcony scene. What? Coming
to bed so late (a bad shot). What scene? She didn't jump or
shoot. in anger. as I could see (so late, so isolate): You
hide from me & I'll hide from you. Wide of the mark. (Was it
a wrong move? for arms, his, to surround.)

Back in the car, luggage stowed, up out of the dead end street,
into highway sun streams in the pines high up, hair tied ... D
with his arm around C, eyes what streams by in the splash of
window frame says: Good idea that firewood in the trunk — did
you see it? See? The whole set, false front, the frame,
go up in flames.

On their sudden (?) split
                    for Al

Noon, once opened, opens gaps where day dwells:
in the back of the head. Misled, lingered or,
led there by accident, it dwells — pristine
bodies of jellyfish tide left. husks. once
opened, scatter then.

                          Could she have
seen him / could i? Stiffen, salt thru walls
washt with a day we thought we lived in,
                                            At
Monterey, mountain of the king, late spring (summer)
we might have noticed the ice plants' last influx
of salt, crystal them ceaselessly & form suns

              (thru prisms
                pristine as
                tears, as what
                stiffens

we know we reflect them.

        ii

Night, any swell of dark weight, watery, shifts
ground, shifts what floats underfoot. to most
mournful sound. Animal lost or missed, or more
simply hunger, fish-calls: a swell lifts one
of them up, nosing for, almost a hairy would,
demand & down.

36

Feel what swims under
surface tension visible to eyes ...

need more than sun. sun on your flesh,
bright hair present blinds the eye, i need,
she did, being met, submerged & wet, the
playful roll of being together. rolls under
in dream as still she slept, i did, our day
light to the walls.
                              At which point
Horizon, breaks down the door. A man, under
the tile-edged lid of sleep, cool, surveys
what day brings. coming & going of town,
his hand, his anger cuts. what part lives
(wind) what must blow

                        It's the knife edge of
transaction wipes their going clean.

        iii

            unmet under night
            liquid of i's the animal is (howl)
            we went on to Carmel, we went
            on

        iv

Leaving them level with the bay. Tracks grass,
broken head that bees pour over, fence &
cannas then. Sign, like a wall prevents:

Old Customs House

        (Pay, pay. His guns
stand off all day, threatening raid at night.

While she, still no response, white, houses quiet
& disuse. & the odour of wooden flooring much
stept on, grows fainter to us under wind & lightshine
hours away, hours on end, by the sea.

bells, the

big
    bronze
carillon to
california

always
passage father
swears by
(little known

              who loves to
              ring them
              all, a

signal safe
arrival
praise a
child makes

music in
eyes' fire

        "works"!

that
anyone
can bring
          (new
worlds to
being

homeward

tan
fields look stranger
rain, clouds, torn
scour
sun settles

worn with our
climbing over
children of hours
eyes) for real under

      high wind
      hawks
      cloud

to be left
moon, a very late
house settles
deer, the grass
bathroom window
waters

highway points
north til east orior rise
at 4 a.m.

then open country under

opulent mountain rain
falls

Vancouver

this house Vera found for us in Dunbar — staid, English, middle-class Vancouver. houses separated by yards of lawn, "shops" trying to look like a village clustered around 2 supermarkets. this place feels so established after our crooked Pigeon Hill house by the tracks (Bloomington), its pokey rooms & roaches — after our yellow foreman's bungalow so close to the earth & the vineyard in Napa. both those places temporary but we *lived* in them. here I feel like we're living in somebody else's house, maybe because we are — somebody else. not "struggling students" anymore, as Al said. now he's a faculty member & I'm a "faculty wife" (part-time English teacher too). it doesn't fit & yet it's what we've worked for, or he has, to return successful — home town boy makes good.

but it's not the same. it's the grip of the establishment we run up against — feeling it in the neighbourhood, feeling it in the department. at the college too, the old guard, even tho it's a brand new psychiatric hospital out at the university. While Fourth Avenue's become a hippy strip, almost, except for the grass boulevards, another Haight. Vancouver growing awkwardly out of its old WASP shell.

November 16/68

Vancouver because I can write more easily here?
because I can be angrier here? this neighbourhood, this city, in some
sense mine

Dubliners.
interred.

that myth of childhood we want to get inside of, recalling old movies we all saw, ball teams or bubble gum wrappers collected, or old hit songs — that sense of a common culture we all shared — that we belonged in a togetherness/ openness not duplicated since: shared interests, common dream goals Al & I shared.

(at root in Kerouac & in Fournier)

how single or solitary we become. having learned to play/beware of games, as the one who was excluded then felt (immigrant kid). no shared jokes weighs, because it means anything given may be a joke & one is 'taken.' no keys to common ground between us.

is it only animals of prey (cats, lions, cougars) curl in comfort after effort (the hunt), curl, purr, lick, enjoy a bodily & self-contained pleasure?

November 20/68

during meditation class tonight someone said the Roshi said our big problem is the "subject/object dichotomy" — meaning? ego sets up walls to think of itself as alone subject, a lonely subject

value of Ponge, his insistence on the *presence* of things, thus objects as subject, of course of the writing but — what would it feel like being shrimp/ plant/butterfly, taking on the conditions of shrimp/plant/butterfly life. *is* he trying for the unknowable, the garden without us?

which has always fascinated me — 'negative capability,' or the seeping of one's consciousness into other, non-self places (but if every imagining of the other is only a projection of the self?), or as Ponge puts it, the invasion of self by things.

44

more than Sartre's stress on consciousness (an only human world) & more than any obligation to merely take account of things — it's the obligation to voice them, in their terms, & from a sense that they exist without us. they don't need us, we need them. just as we need to voice them — pushing the limits of what we know/ what we can voice —

must be what the Roshi meant, that we exist in all things, us as makers of the real, which exists in *our* eyes, ears, etc. we make (up) the universe in that sense.

to return to it, the unknowability of the world that gets us — no other evidence than what our senses give, corroborated by information from others (language, the world is, finally). as far as we know: we realize, trees don't. do we exist as crossroads of recognition for things/persons which appear, briefly transparent in all their inter-connectedness, & then disappear into individual & unknowable opacity again? things flame in us, as words do. things flame in us as words.

December 27/68

now 23 weeks pregnant, 5 months

getting awkward. have got to keep doing excercises, keep limber. (feeling oppressed? feeling? should have been keeping track all along.)

feeling lonely, more cut off from Al than almost any other time. except he seems to grow more interested as I grow bigger (& we can feel the baby move now). movements, 1st felt in dentist's chair, like very slight shifting movements, bubbles as Donna said but not long bubbles, very brief. grew til now he kicks, it feels like, sometimes almost as if hiccups — rhythmic, twitches.

feelings of being 'put upon,' 'put out' certainly as I grow less able to do the things I've always done: a matter of movement, quickness. at 1st the fact that I couldn't drink bothered me: beer parlour or whatever, all I prided myself on, keeping up with Al & the men, the camaraderie etc. this is shattering, that I am just like other women, subject to the same "failings" & the lack of energy at 4 months, that I couldn't both write & teach.

thoughts keep coming to mind, if I can follow all tracks — why couldn't I write? complained of not feeling still centre in myself any longer, because invaded by strange (alien) growth? felt irritable, weepy, *victimized.* but it's not as if the baby feels like an alien inside me: rather i feel protective toward it (this sense grows) & after 1st movements that I was sure gradually were *it,* not my own gas bubbles or whatever, a new worry every time I didn't feel it for a day or so.

now i can't sleep all night, wake & go pee. street lamp shines thru glass inserts by the front door down the hall (shining off snow these last few Xmas nights) — 'still of the night' — myself alone & cold bathroom tiles underfoot. but not alone — don't even mind really — like keeping a secret? I suppose lonely women feel most elated by this secret company.

coming into the sense now of wanting to use perfume, bath powder, col-oured oils. & later, after it's over, wanting to dress up in sleek dresses — that all these things I disliked now have rime & reason, as if I'm coming into my rightful femininity. & maybe that's why women have wanted these things, after all the *work,* all the organic & animal labour.

sometimes I look "beautiful" ("radiant"? clear-skinned anyway, & clear-eyed. my hair's growing, after the initial falling-out. & less pimples). & sometimes I just look dragged-out, red-rimmed around the eyes, pinched. sometimes I feel a new kind of female pride or sureness, which is also dangerous because I grow smug & risk myself less in conversation. feel then as if just being is enough.

here

wings it
glues light
green shows thru

      (birds
         inland reflectors

out to sea
your longing move
in on itself
      /waves

aqueous humour steep
what shines in
your window

      (our perceptions, do
         birds indicate our weather?

best perhaps to
split you said
eyes not yours not
explicable
      in space
birds traverse

nothing, we
hang on by gravitation the
  attracted body's

eyes lips ears remember

weight & texture of
your head
       (winging, what

no map, no passing eye can
discover

postcard from a distance
                              for D.

would the kookaburra, some
exotic, crest, all
zebra feathered, beak
too curved for

                    humming bird's
                    thought 'honey birds'

in the well of some
profuse
bruise

masquerade?

no answers white
distance lies
its long neck tokens

                    'not well'
                    not much more than
                    not

                    thunderbird or
                    woodpecker would
                    peck

dry blood?
rust?
nevertheless

its black eye speaks
too proud for words

reading

rain ge
rainiums
dried out

shrouds

fog's dis
embody stalks

if trees, dilute
solutions of them
selves salvage

limits of
a ten
        sion

can eye
appraise what
fog says

only now

delta

faces the
surface of
water

make rain seas
in the world maintain
equilibrium equals

balance, comment, rushing
mountain streams or plain
ditches on the
dyke road

skinny & feminine under
rain hats hide
(rushes, rushing odour of
cabbage)
          eyes only
hands pluck cut
center from floral
decay

     its smell of
flower stem left
forever in
fetid vase

you said our
car never
gets
stuck

O miz estrus

who rides composed, immigrant to this city,
longtime resident. in shadow, shallow (who knows?
nothing of tides.

o miz estrus who rides, whose mouth is
the mouth of rockcod, rocked, open & shut down avenues of
sun, bus on big tires braking
who rests, who swallows (air)
light, mouth of onions & goodday uttered late absorbed
in fading, deeper than rust in photograph ...

whose nights leak out in brush raccoons reveal each raid
their brief history of blood ...

whose pads &
tailored blouse & nether panties soak in the heat of
bus upholstery, sun going down, going home, counts
on revolutions of meter, amount of water,   whose gold
sleeps under her bed in a chinese coffer ...

& stores the moon
(against what catastrophe?
o miz wellwrapt
shadow of a shadow, mum,   the sun ... infuses window
(honey) widening, opened on clover stir, a breeze, a
tide of grasses barefoot o
your hands mutter & dart,
rockcod in the shadow of your thighs, while faces outside
unseen, matted, lions roar

in revolution, revels of the
SUN ...

merci

a few light flakes
a form of en
coding, calling
up the nth
limit
    (mine

    .   .

your car wheels slip
in time

's my rime against
the grain

    .   .

begin again:
warm-up is imminent
the rain

i said i like
snow

transforms all
matter of things
    (weights wings, erases
territory

    .   .

whose fence?

under the impact of
light merriment

            .   .

gloves
mercifully clothe
cold hands
                demand some
                . *recompense*

am i wrong
to see it so
mercenary?

        .   .

your small acts
flakes
            round me fall
soften the outline of
my suspicion

bearing
no ill will you
easily shift into

snow bank, no
bank on some
limit 'like'

likes snowing
under
            /you
do too.

Long time coming

Sea hood, snail, born with a caul on his head,
tumbles in weedy medium of now. Semen falls as
dizziness. sink back to head tail snail objects. weeds to catch at his shell like hair,
cilia he puts his foot on now grabs hold. eye
feeling thru rain

                        am not down. water runs down
the windowpane i face. disaffections. might order
a new order as water waves its snail pace ...

snared in a diver's hold. i come up for breath.
around & over our heads the sound of moss fingers
our eaves. melt. snow purple at eyes' level
swallows from view. two. in a cell. i keep coming
up for breath, crackle of light fragments, genes.
help

    '' as if there were anything but''

love orders another order of mosses, snows, in all
this iridescent coal.

Missed meaning

        eyes shimmy in their fire sight —
your sign or theirs? trust like *tresor* or rust a
foreign element that ghosts

        waver over. their left
shoulders wound like salt (luck failed, by my distrust).
your eyes' hot looks: as to the rest of you? composed,
divining those things called *escarbilles,* not cinders
clinkers rocks or ...
        some subtler thing, fished from under
ash of eyes minus any kind of conscious stare, just
there in their heat hardly tears or ex-tensions of the
wood ...
    (would)
        burn for what, love? entered with the
state entrusted meant: trust that hands lay up. (spark)
where neither moth nor rust doth ...

        reserve:
that part of coal which having escaped combustion rests
mixed up with ash

        but, still nameless, these spend them
selves. ember? glow still in ash distilled rise (rain)
unquenchable . eyes . outside of signals?

    do you know them?

                              kin, i thought,
create of fire, scorpions or flame-inhabiting salamanders,
do not themselves burn.

                         ah *escarbille* down to (snake eyes)
these original heat-tears.

                         moon moon

                    eyes at the
                    page, hand

                    wobbles its
                    shadow it's

                    cast
                         (broke
                    spells

                    who's eyes to
                    see by?

largely sea

at, eye
cloud your
silence casts

   a light

spray sea
islands us
out of the waves'
crash we stand

       stranded

       pebbles stript
       of liquid
       r's l's roar

       how one word cast

light, define
in midst of a
(mist a
deafening
sound

       this man
       bows out

          taub, deaf
           or stupid
          dau-, dead

                              daubs unreceptive to
                              impressions, blind

          in a fume i'm left
          to smoke
          your absence out

          beyond rocks can't
          make mental categories
          stick
                    (your agates don't
                    count

          ī*g* land, *ē*a
          land, not water, eye
          frays us just
          so far see
          what can't be
          made out

                    frei, free

          belonging to
          one's own
          daufr
                tho that be

          listen, just one
             pebble
          pickt up, suckt
          cuts both ways:

no savour without taste
no salt but sweat, yours
or mine to make

a little noise.

Getting there

carp, carp on, tooth ... biting at rain. almost to an ache,
city-way the salmon, gliding, never feel it on their
surface, make it thanks to rivers.

> linked hands or gills,
gulp at the air where air caresses our strange backs, bellies
submerged successful, system the fish move in,

> as that day
winter moved into the lake, fingers, selves all bracken
where they used to slink, hooks deserted now. mysterious
fish swim further downlake, deeper ...

> carp stay. always
that tooth aggressive into the air, just piercing gum ...

carp on they say, talkative, females of the race, a genius
characterized by, rise to the occasion, words, vacuous as
kites. race the air currents tug at strings for opening
mouths, gulp, air tails are laid in. as i'm jealous of her,
she-fish, her ease. myself divest of aches, pain, rain's

a festival the way it gentles us now, we bend in to see
the sky's immense racks of rainwear,

> naked our skins swim
this element, those kites, paper, shouting the wet air ...

bird of passage

thaw begins
   tonight
eaves drip in
cessant
     ring

wind
bell spring's
brought
    forward in time

         this
         bird

         dive bird
         nestle why
         stop? nested
         under the eave of
         flesh or

strong wet bird swims

         in me
         turned as i am against
         your anonymous hip
         in sleep some
         cliff
         must be
         negotiated

  /swallow

eave swallows cliff
passerine
                which i thought meant
passing as passenger
sails thru an isthmus
time does not constrict

helpless

constriction in my
throat, seeing the
picture of
oil slick bird "will
die"
        fixt
its feathers mock
coming out of yolk

                this
                black
                stuff

fix of its own
birth?

so a month's
accumulation of
tears into
icicles, vesicles

leaves roof in
cessant
            release

                    /can be

nothing more than
alone, urine passt
warm
      squat by the
window's cold

only to lie:
        "alone"
        not alone, not

ceasing its skim
in serous
medium, light as
air to us
gravity bound

head over heels or
wing
      /bones supplied
to test its limits

        (passage?
        passing
        passenger

temporary nest
high in the air
hirundinidae
        hirondelle in
"graceful
flight & regular
migration"

fathered by a bird too
sought definition for

            its passage
            bird of
            sea, bird of passage or

''a rolling stone''

jumps in the womb for
joy?
            of recognition, cog
nition, knowing
whence sound came
a rhythm
                        per
vades, rocking
waves under the face of
his)
            ''fight

            to be heard over
            the din''
                        we are all
            born in
            risk
                        mute

cliff

i cannot grasp
your sound . breath . stone
you turn dumb & will
not speak
                        of what sticks at
                        feathering

                    uneasy nest
                    unease, a
                    restlessness

tonight
            drips in
passing in
return perhaps
light airs, we
begin
            'again'

under

apple, wind, wild
sea moves
on itself out

shift
       slips

in the air's a motion
sigh hurled, window

open at bottom ships
cool

it isn't, or it can't be just the weather — he feels trapped — "nowhere to drive" after all those country roads in Napa — but he knows there's the Valley here, the delta — it's not that

he feels he can't move/act, has nowhere to go at work — trapped in department politics, the power struggle

he feels stuck & he can't move out of it to talk about it

perception — to transcribe directly as Robbe-Grillet does, as if eye were a camera, phenomenological

       relief from the subjective (unreliable) where falsehoods are indistinguishable from the real (self-deception — language *provides* for it)

    or as Anne Minor says: "the narrator seeks to convince himself of his own objectivity' (because it is his objectivity that places him in a world of objects equally solid, accountable) — Morrissette speaks of R-G's "realism of presence"

ok, R-G gets us on the scene by straight description (accounting), avoids speaking of the psychological, the introspective. Ponge gets into a hypothetical psychology of things (accounting *for*), or at least applies our psychology to them (trees seeking to cover the world in a vomit of green, etc) — desires, goals, projects, & defences — how it would be to be a tree. & ends up getting us present in language.

Jealousy works but it's a stylized reality. one's presence is not marked only by what one sees — a 'state of mind' is a place, permeates environment (*how* it is perceived) & event — is told in that talking to oneself that goes on incessantly (whether false or true). but the sensation of time in R-G feels accurate to me: associative collage of present, past, & (possible) future, also permeated by memory

like listening to Van Morrison's "TB Sheets" which brought back, as if I had walked into that living room, the state of mind I was in in Napa listening to the same song: strong as a taste, a psychic taste (Proust)

January 29/69

the *simultaneity* of experience (so many elements occurring in conscious-ness at once) — the rapidity of conscious movement (of what appears in "lime light" — one thought leading to the next — or being called up by the preceding — it is not a linear extension but much more a spiralling —

the foci are like complexes (light rings) — they expand & shade into one another

January 31/69

difficult to locate the writing in public places, dept. store or any aspect of city, it's the density of sensations — the writing becomes caricature (just the most obvious characteristics pickt up)

approach it on a language level:
vocabulary, its range: snow as collective experience, use cutups from *Prov-*
ince accounts of drifts in Sumas Prairie, etc — milk trucks — people on their
rounds (rings)

so far have got their resistance to each other based on their different
attitudes to snow — & the snow — outering vs inner dwelling

next perhaps
should be the rounds & snow passages (her attempt to see a shared reality)
while he? pursues his daily things, driving to work, smoking, music — her
jealousy (what is he really thinking of? or her insecurity)

working towards a vision of community (with things & people)
        vs isolation

_____ reality is synchronic _____

the writing is basically trying to tell the way it is — part recording what's
there & part voicing a state of mind (each does dwell inside his/her head,
sees out from there) essentially circular

but feel need in "telling a story" to
work towards some "climax", which means imposing a "plot-line" no
matter how minimal?

the "plot-line" is the drift, which circles back on itself
while still moving towards some recognition — this rather than a plotted
crescendo of conflict & resolution. resistance is part of her daily where-it-is
anyhow & part of basic differences between self & other. not a developing
line, so there can be no solution to it (& in this sense it is not a "problem,"
not the story's anyhow).

Kelly said I'm drawn to those men who deal with "the outer processes of intellect" & fear the "vulvary darks of the mind." this probably so – a fear I share with Al? of the mother, of being suffocated in the dark?

what draws me is the light as a saving irradiation – appearance, *parēre* – to come forth, be visible – dark things faced & named
– chaos of feelings below words (as fear) threatens to overcome. but to speak is to recognize, to see.

the dark & the unknown, that which we are born out of. we talk about being born & not about being (made) dead – we say we die & yet we don't say we born or bear (ourselves). infant at mercy of the uterine muscle which expels it & the hard walls of the birth canal which, threatening to close in, yet pass it thru the ring of the cervix, out. the uterus, the placenta, decide when to thrust it out – & yet, coming forth into the light the child suddenly is, appears to us – an other, recognized as itself, making its own appearance into the world.

March 13/69

'into the world'

rings within rings (eco-logical or atomic) (outward & inward)

(house is my environment these days)

(as I am a house for — her/him?)

or more like spheres, as the japanese ball, inner nut of one
    forming outer husk of next

                                    ⌐ cutting edge: what matters?
matter (incarnate) in what's the matter?
                                    ∟ primary stuff for building (rings)

mater (mother) in matter

what is a story? why write a story?

        historein — inquire into, relate
        idein — to see
        vīdyā — knowledge: to see

to see, to understand the relations

March 20/69

his accusation is against my withdrawal into "unreal" world of only-house
— move on to celebration, in advance, of world of connexions, both child &
us

(the revolutionary? belly of the whale

the moving point . anger

matter is opaque — mother is secret (inarticulate) — source of smothering yet
skin as window (that's the solution): Lennart Nilsson's photos of embryo
growing inside

the writing takes so long because it is attempting to get the whole field of
consciousness (*not* linear logic) of any given 'i' or 'he' — the process of
thinking is not logical, but the deepest reasons for action are tied to complexes of feeling not postulates of thought.

the whole field must be brought forward, or as much as possible, to understand a point of view.

aversion, a turning away — as he turns from me & from the city into himself
— his aversion to his situation between both departments so intense he will
look for another job, the States again. he says this is a backwater, out of the
mainstream which runs south (as always). that he has a good chance of a job
at Wisconsin. what's at Wisconsin? says we'll look for a farmhouse, live in
the country again. he brightens, he can make it seem real to me. but it feels
like a recurring dream, this search for somewhere to put down roots — just
when i begin to feel mine tangled here in the roots of the city.

this afternoon's dream — Al at work, house quiet, sun bright after cloudy morning & in my dream a stillness too. I remember beginning to feel the head in vagina, inevitably, quietly — a very sensual feeling — & thinking I should phone someone. got up & the light was darkening around supper-time — our street lined with cherry trees, some a very dark pink (vivid as may) against the dusk, others like one in front of our house, a lighter pink — the lawns that strange brilliant green (is it the light of sun behind cloud at evening, a bright sun, so that only the surface dazzle is gone & the light still stands in things, they give off their own high-saturation but surface-darkened colour?) & there was an orange sanitation truck moving slowly down the street & boys were lopping off lower limbs wreathed in flowers, the whole tree swarming with excited shouting boys & the men were letting them keep the limbs.

        after those colours the day seemed dull & ordinary. feeling as of all closing in aperture of camera, going down towards the dark. if a death dream, most tranquil.

        connected somehow with Kanaka Ran-cherie which I thought should be title of the Vancouver poems book — these visitations from the past. (there once *was* a tree in front of this house, but were there ever cherry trees down this street?) it is the lush sensuality (oriental) that is the constant note of these poems

        & what were the Hawaiians doing here? were there also Japanese? Morely, 32, "A higgledy-piggledy settlement of Indians, Kanaka & Scandinavian deserters from the sailing ships & 'busted' refugees from the gold mines grew up around the mill & provided his labor force." Stamp's Mill, beginning of the city. & p. 41, Raymur's taking it over, 1869 "whereupon the conglomeration of male, female & infant Kanakas, Indians & roustabouts was forthwith banished, with their cows, chickens, pigs, cats & dogs. A company bunkhouse was provided for single men & the happy-go-lucky Kanakas retired to the farthest reaches of Coal Harbour, where their settlement became known as the Kanaka Rancherie or, alternatively, the Cherry Orchard, for in time its cherry trees became one of the springtime sights of the inlet."

April 30/69

impatience — peripheral attention to anything needing more, such as writing letters. difficult to settle to anything, or give account of where I'm at — perpetually about to walk thru the door.

tension delays uterine contractions? so many signs: baby's inactivity during day, energy lately (15 block walk yesterday that I enjoyed — tranquillity of gardens, old people's lives glimpsed thru windows), movement at head of cunt, strange, like period starting but nothing comes. & then contractions every evening starting about 5:00, in response to baby's movements. muscle spasms in buttocks, evenings, difficult to sit still for any length of time. pangs of sudden depression when I realize, my god, *three* weeks overdue. but mostly I move from day to day, no overview. sleeping afternoons with nightmares, & mornings after dawn. wake up feeling sick with hunger but no appetite. my god, it all sounds neurotic — hanging onto the baby out of fear? that it won't be perfect, that I'm into something I can't deal with, that once the baby's out it's so vulnerable to illness, accident — stay in there where it's warm. sometimes unreal sense there's no baby at all. things in the room gathering dust.

Rings
for Kit

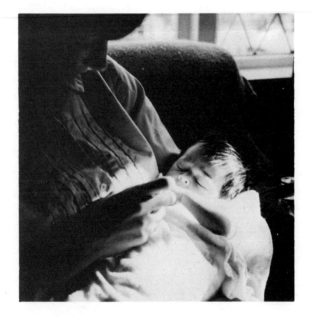

Rings, i.

       Like a stone. My what's the matter? dropt as
mothering smothered by the snowy silence, yours. Me?
the morning? or?
               Metal clangs in zero weather cold hands
make. A jangling of rings, loose. Sky does not begin
today. Disguising offwhite of what the ground is. falling.
away from us.

         ... will look up, stare as if (Why do you make
so much noise? Slurping coffee he objects to. What if
it's pleasure? Forgot. Noise occupies a room already
occupied by

       Snow, as silence,

              one of the first things (white
rabbits, or hares & rabbits, which?) It's snowing. Yes
(that muffle light peculiar to) Pleased? He knows i always
am. Don't sound so pleased about it. Inevitable as the
weather we wake up to. Cold stare, snap, hair. Mute.
Waking so slow coffee seethes. I sit here, seething. Object.
Not alone but occupied, & large. That seething movement's
him? Objects, at sea within me, unseen medium thru which
chemicals reach
        Not high & dry as coffee grounds us waking
agitated. Do i make it up? this cold within him. Nerve ends
replacing what i know, or what i know he says. The moments,
delimited now, grow into hours he doesn't move toward me in,
could be, just, waking up.
        That he said after i had so carefully
boiled it after the percolator broke, something strong to

wake up to i said, There's more coffee in the pot. That stuff?
What 'stuff'? What did you do to it, BOIL it?

                                        Makes it incredible.
That i did, just that. That's how some men like their coffee.
The answer to that is, how would you know?

                                        Snow. Inhabits a
room, a silent, blanket. he can't stand. windows. smothering.
light flakes lower themselves, no wind so, begin to eddy but
the eye, looking out, sees them suspend in thickets — thicker
i grow, looking more globular & still. Not stone but silent
plummeting slow descent of white. Or who knows what form it
takes in that liquid, fishtailed small frog swimming, shut
eyes blurred by water. soft. touch

                                        his hand, say —
It's only snow. But he, what're you talking about? not to
assume. His anger his, or, gets up to look at, his right to
move is what. Bald tires & metal merged with snow on top.
He's thinking, weekend, shit, how to get out? & no one's
even tried, the bankedup cars immobile, zigzag path across
white (grass) the only evidence of any moving body...
                                        news-
paper boy. Must have been up at 5:30 this morning, anyway
still dark when i saw him. & want to say, how, tell you that
moment? Down our hall's perspective, old posters, yours, &
family tree, phonograph ad, no, sidetrack ... At night only
illumined inroads of light (from) street burning still thru
glass. untimed. unchecked. Felt like i was trespassing our
hall this hour & all hours inhabited by outer ... movement,
Caught movement first then, must have been the tail end of his
swing, the second bag up across his back, Pause, that
lonely, even lordly stance — legs braced solid against the
weight, stare (for breath?) down HIS street, not knowing

anyone else ...

        Hmm. Punctuates blank silence only as you leave,
for light? ashtray? I haven't clearly explained. Or even
why? Snow. had something to do with the public street. Door
opening cold, air, ankles. You, a clearer view of the car?
Silent, silence off the street. Of course, newspaper. step.
shaking snow. shut. to living room or here? There.

Well, so what is coffee grounds for? edginess. Still warm
in the cup when circled swirls dis/content, what can't be
strained out. sludge you'd call it, slush. Or think you'd call.
It always turns to slush. How can i be taken in, each time
by the 'matter' of?

        (Mothering hindsight, that voice. But i'm
as much at sea as fish tailed thing, waiting for whatever clue
(dumb, hurts) observing ... Your anger carefully cut off here
as the door is shut.

        Your anger's at the snow? or at this
strangeness (mine) snow also creates — a cover. no clarity.
or long view to

        Ah miles of country road you're wanting, beer,
sunshine, sage. Moving anywhere at any junction's chance (Lost
Gap, Last Chance) of getting lost, of moving off the map.
        I'm
lost already. You'd shrug, word games. Or melodrama's badly
contained elements. Your discontent, feeling contained here.
Or mine? My nerve ends stretch. I read too much in your words,
read silences where there is nothing to say, to be said, to be
read. in,
        What is it, half an hour to Blaine? as blatant
understatement, your need to get out. Mudflats & smuggled quarts.
That's not country, that taverntown. You stare. Because what?
i forgot country music maybe, girls & beer (i can't drink with)

who lean, cigarette smoke stock in trade (i make a bad melodrama)
so lean, your eyes moving up (i'm getting wide, solid here) could
dance if she would (if you would), moves off alone & liking it —

A good match, driving, snaps it. Nowhere. Irritable in this
(it moves) opposing your restiveness with increased roots,
weight. (Wait. Footloose, who used to be? Wind driven down
the beach yelling, Run, run

                 to you in the other room.
Newspaper face, newspaper up & you behind it do not move or
register my coming. (Say) There's more ... Hmm. (dumb, forgot.
why slide into motherly offer of stores? as if such smoothing-
over weren't transparent.
                Say it stays. dumb. opaque. grey.
sticks at landmarks, erases lawn edge. steps. foundations. what
lies to be plowed thru. to get at, out. Our car lies furred
to the snowbank. bald tires. You ignore the whimsy. Who
expects to get thru winter on tires like that? Something's
got to give (our street tilts, our horizon does. while eye,
stand at the window, frozen.
                You'll just have to cut down.
'You.' as if i do all the eating ('for 2'). How'd you like
beans every night? Sure.
                So our ground, even the ground's
dispersed. Knows very well, we both do ... No matter (ANY
intrusion of supposition). When he stands so dense words won't.
penetrate.

        Cut thru to the other room. Snow here too at all
the windows blankets an inner impasse. Why not say i'm angry?
(was it a small thing? where do i end & you begin? what is
small?

Dust settles, sediments the table saturate with, as
outside, small bits or flakes. Time passes. more exactly increments its weight. hands clenched, eyes tight shut. or open
sometimes in the dark. strange. survival's based solely on
weight.

      & weather, inside or out, whether anyone is. skin.
flakes off the cats. dust falling. hair in eye or hand closeup
skin leaded like some windowpane opaque. is old. 'you want to
stay home all the time.' No, i need to feel at home here at
impenetrable skin.

Mother is inarticulate dark?

Smothering?

      No. Get water walk to the kitchen. Pot still
pool bits of oatmeal float in. floats in body temperature
within, soft skin, covered with a down to which some wax
adheres, lardlike, secretion. a photograph filtered thru its
rim (hand's): light, thru membrane & water.

                    Remember? ways
of breaking thru (waves) windows are: the front room's sun!

Kicks, suddenly unaccountable unseen, make their way felt thru
skin anyway a fact beginning. Heat. Pierces glass (cold)
irradiating skin, water, wood. & snow crust isolate in crystal
flake like mica or micro-point all joined uncountable thousands
& one-cell, each a room, internal, order in time runs

                                  on, in
me, pierced, clouds uncountably moving body works, his light
foot within.

      & out? Coming in & going out, he wants to break
thru, into the flow memory brings, uncalled for

83

              ... can i?

flickering at the doors, suspended *(long distance, information, ...)*
amber wheels lamps these 6 years unchanged *(help me, information,*
get ...) must of dark heads ring . table's wet mark from wet
bottom of glasses *(in touch with my....)* thru all this sound *(mari)*
make sense of what's been *(... only 6 years old,* mari *...)* someone
laughing *(... just a half a mile from ...)* his room's a crowd
(the mississippi bridge ....)

                  redbuds in spring red canyon down
thru which ... in lampdark light glitters, fitful, his voice
picks at word/ sound descends, that one lost town we never
could find, he says, & forgets the name of brownstown, brown
county, no. the lost one, gosport. with stone houses never
stopt at, steinsville. by land. (& missed.) he is surrounded
by hands, voices picking for, lost note, name all recognize
in time (glossed over) *we,*

                the single sound a moment he will
                be in

                not the newspaper he's with-
drawn behind, that cover temporary only, Well
                    What? Sun's out,
look. You do look. warmer. So it is.

Rings, ii

        I'm goin ta
        Move up to the
        Country, babe,'n
        Paint my mail
            box blue

                        wink, is one wink,
two, blue one he said never does blink out, too much in music
to, see it. Light. Create: fern raising carboniferous shadows
cave we're into. Bob on his back does stare at. us under.
the street may be a thousand light years curtains don't reach,
not quite, from here. Don't want to, move, heavy going like a
stone, sits
        Rocking. Eases its bulk, hardly separate tho i
envelop. cave i make, my flesh weight his movement thru, water
kicks, independent of, the room? my thought? all ringed in
smoke (curtains) shift. through us. What we live, this air
thick with its changing, colours his, father's face far from
thought of it, cued to sound, the knob, 2 knobs turning slowly.
bass creeps further into the room, insistent. roots. tree sound.
Heart beats (mine must be for him a constant ambience, yes,
recording, over & over) one trunk we leaf up thru, this smoke
a mist, a mystification, leaves us
                  Visible from outside? Is it
the street light seeps so cold, a whiter outer light ... recall
sidewalk's flat extent, spent, dead underfoot infinite all
those roots bones paved over, not suffered to reach daylight,
or night. Light. Car glides in, idles, lights off just outside.
Who is that?
        (outered)
            What? That car ...

effects, out of the
mist, break-up now as Bob, quivering more on the outside, finger
tip, to feet too. Al: she always does this. But we all (curtains
don't meet) to that gap & the station wagon seen now under the
tree has stopt, engine off, doors open & the kids removing bottles,
one carton, two, three ... more, laying them martialled under the
tree's leaf spattered light. What are they? Empties. What are
these kids? & the man himself removing the last as they troop
upstairs. We have screwy neighbours Al says. In the dead of
night, taking empties IN? Bob: what do they drink? Not beer,
pop. Sugar high teenager laid out on lounge at back under the
appletree, classic, never looks over fence, or not obviously,
transistor fed torso thin in swim trunks ...

                        & the cool
wind blows. anticipating summer. it is all in the head, some
overriding need to make it so. in advance, ahead of time. Al,
yanking the curtains closed. Bob sees at once, it comes in the
sides, laughing. That's ok. Me: but it comes in 2 places now.
Al: well damn it which do you want? Bob exults, why don't you
open them all the way let it all hang out. Al: the lights,
they'd know, what kind of freaks live here. Those particular
little houses lockt, particles all, cut off from the silent, the
unused street flow, outside our enclosed & cavernous selves.
Maybe they'll think you keep you christmas tree up a long time.
Into March? Or think it's colour tv. Some kind of aquarium.
Home movie.
        No, there's no doubt. freaks. They don't cut their
grass, wash their car, hang proper curtains. Cut the curtains!

                             Back,
back into the room we circle, It rings us. No, grows out of our
heads like the fern in carboniferous light. Smoke. An age since.
Yes.

Who compose themselves on the floor, anticipant. limbs a
kind of compact ... Wait: Bob: scotch. you want some? Yes.
Happy funny-man gait thru the door. Al lost in selecting what?
to order the atmosphere, they both do, vying, now this, wait,
dig this, any requests AFTER blood sweat & tears? Who after all
arranged the lights, a constant flicker to pursue (out of the
corners of our eyes) a slight engagement, one blue light, blue
dream —
    prospect shut. the risk you teach me, want to say, of reaching
you. Just there's the gap (rocking, tho i will, do now move down to

Carpet rough like dry grass & you, compact against the music
treelike, branching into all corners, broadleafed sound of
tropical rain, tapping the dried stems leaves down, pack it
into the player's you emptied, functional, use of what's at
hand. As Bob, apart, would roll his own — getting the scotch,
clown sloppy, so high, higher than we even begin. Enthusiasm's
not clumsy, no, to fly at certain pitch, That sound, wow, that
cut ... looselimbed, HIS sound, HIS memory (remember, standing in
snowsuit armstiff, chuckle, remember?) The spill diffuses in
widening rings on the carpet we all now sit in, blotches of
colour, blooms, or even cockatoos jute scratches, rough but,
as he says, sucks up scotch well enough.

       Gonna / move up *to the /*
country, Suddenly Al, that funny toneless voice he never hears
himself in, singing, elsewhere. Bob's immediate long toke
as if ribs would cave out. I'm getting it from the atmosphere
this room expires, slowly, masses of hot air, ferny devil's club
we used to brush by...
     3 of us sitting in cave furry on skin
mind meets, curious, contact ...
       his fingers handing it are thin,
definite, care i take it. sharp breath of green plants then,
their very fibre. on to him, so well known he's unaware, head

down, beating into the sound. Nudge. Without a glance, knowing
who gives it, why, there is no doubt. The way he takes short
cool drags, sieving it through. Always 2 ways, 2 &

                                                me in the
middle suddenly holding a fourth. Who? Anything like that ghostly
shaking down of cuffs, a gambler, way he passes it declarative
to Bob?

           Hard to imagine what he (she) carries of each of us
&, there, a trap, into maternal forcing, how you force a tree,
no. Nobody but himself. & in due time, when (he). Then he?
because i want to understand HIM better? easier to have a girl.
for him. me? Not, surely not, the victorian hangup on bed
weeping, 'she will have to go thru what i did.'

                                             (so, a little fear?

It's only his foot caught under my ribcage & kicking. Can
feel the ridge of muscle outlined there. Got to move up.
Beginning to get that feeling my whole flesh has slipt down
on its bones doubled up. But then, up there i'd be removed
Mother rocking. complacent. or placid, deeply satisfied somewhere
inside. but not enough.

                       Is that it?   Not wanting to be
where i am: woman, to follow her, my own mother. Or too much
wanting more – know how THEY feel. It's a man's world,
she said. (Got to stand up in.) World? Happens there, out
there. Not here? Here's a world between us 3, not off the
top of my head. Trouble is, i stood up poked my head thru the
roof ...

                 Wow: Bob, lying on his back & laughing up.
What's it like up there?

                 Very high thin air, i say, maybe the
stratosphere (but not high, i'm not, high, not light enough. Only
he's laughing gentle with me, higher, at, together at it, that

stratosphere. To Al: she is so stoned, laughing, so stoned he
thinks *i* am, laughing at it as i do at his most gentle laughter.
that's ok. to himself it is, ok.

And Al's smiling crosslegged,
sits there still, untranslatable. smile has nothing to do with it,
nodding, into the music, yes he knows, or more like how like Bob
making us be the way he does in his world, its hazy summer burning
perspective. Al still small lost prospect, compact, blue light,
refuses to be drawn in, nodding with the
                                    living with the animals

frogs, crickets, morning outside, pulled outside to the shadow
orchards, hay, the morning glories' wake up, squealing, is a
nanny goat or tires up the gravel, wheeling to a halt the, truck
breaks into ... hello, hello *house in the country* blue, glory,
garbage can lid crashing, heel in the grass, hill he will be
there with him, getting off the, blue truck doors left open ...

That is some cut!

            Were they? i mean was he? back in those hills,
thought it Bob then, Ed, still 3. frogs or crickets sing in
dry grass night thick & smelling so much, hay, a touch of
moisture brings. warm, those rounded hills felt good to stride
over, ride over. his backroads & wild junctions only he remembered,
was a measure of himself there. That you could, he said,
do what you would ... move
                        as we did, around each other more
freely, more, open with ourselves in the open

                              (so why here
this, these curtains, dark, & only the small blue light? saying

... the other night at the, at that place on Fourth. you know,

off Maple (red, candlelight in red glass colours). It was
raining out. You go downstairs off the street. It isn't
big (sound everywhere, we sat so close, all did, to the band
thought he'd jump right out of my skin). Heavy ends, he says,
you should've seen 'em, 6 foot at least, guitar (bass), one
with a preacher's hat, oldtime country. Bridge. The Floating
Bridge. That's it. A brassy sound. declarative. the way they
stand so there, their music does, occur in our heads & take us
in as sign, that one, that emblem of the preacher's trade (& his
black cowboy shirt) hellfire. Heavy act? The cat on the
left, mean-looking, scar, he never smiled.

                                        Image to outer what
(Bob, standing arms out, kid in snowsuit) what's at heart?

& if it's dark at heart & the outering only an empty act, a
gesture played, as if it were the, heart?

                                        If the dark is
equally true, then why speak out at all?

                              Said it & heard the
words fall in between (bridge?) how explain it doesn't even
say now, said, what i intended. Al gets up to play a record
(play?) decisive:

                    It all depends on the temperature. What?
It does (come thru whether you believe he meant). Everything's
in heat.

                Realized what i said: my world, a suppressed
excitement earth intoxicates. these blossoms. this the world he
comes into, coming into light.

                              i can't tell him, express what
runs thru me. heat. fever even as natural. His energy to act
a cooler thing, blue light he sets up, the set up, changing
records now, sustaining, after my mis-fire, the cool mood to
move on, reach out to Bob,

You ought to hear them before they
leave. Tonight. Beer there? Don't know (he does, coffee mugs.)
But first ... toke, scotch, smoke. Always to be off while i stay
unasked (unfair, don't really want to go). He smiles over (that
well known song i know is the last) to allay it, to have me think
it's for Bob he likes to (they both do) end with a beer
& a talk. You know. (i do.)

So meanwhile the room, shadow bits
of fern above us, mirrored fronds trailing, dead ends on the
hearth, rug, leafed & flowered, stays (me turning in, it's time
yes, to sleep, dream out to a larger space) in the meanwhile in
the man's voice, Who? Bob: you never do remember, "the cool
room." Oh, that's who. Man, that is such a great cut. Nameless
his voice fills the room, roots thru flesh/ time/ who (will have
heard this song, turn to, still his crying?
So long, small kiss,
be back. Jacket, last gulp of scotch, where's that lighter? We
can just make it before closing time. Bob on the front porch
swinging his arms. &, so i be not hurt, kiss again, & the light,
street light pouring in.

Rings, iii.

And the bath is a river, in the quiet, i bring only candle
light, in the corner by the faucet, shadows leaping, steam.
& the window. Outside a fresh wind is frothing the apple tree,
its own river streaming, round the house,
                              like a dream,
There is no story only the telling with no end in view or,
born headfirst, you start at the beginning & work backwards.

It was a dream, a report in the newspaper Norman was reading
(it was reported of him telling) he was born in the small
house / shack at the back of 443 Windsor (the street where
we lived — it must have been in the 100's) a big old tree,
dust, & the dilapidation of the main house where they later
lived, all this against a very blue sky that belonged to the
girl the paper said had come out to the coast for health reasons
& stayed, fell in love with the mountains & sea & made frequent
trips by ferry to the island
                    (& Al was on the phone i was
saying but feel the ribs of the baby you can feel them in me
(ribs? his or mine? contractions of muscle, something muscly
& unborn
            that she had in some way redeemed him, he painted
for her or whatever he did that was to make the paper report
his beginning.

             & when i woke up i remembered that Norman had
drowned in a river in the interior in his teens. But not before
i'd thought the past is still alive & grows itself so easily
i must set it down, pre-dawn of a sunny day, Wet, birds in the
half dark singing, trees only just beginning to unfold their
leaves ...

the sea, ferry she was on, small, crossing it, the
sea he looked down on, was the ease of his telling it, where
he is.
    In the bath a sea my belly floats in, i float
relieved of his weight — he floats within. & the genetic
stream winds backward in him, unknown, son of a father once
fathered.

    Tell him, in the bath in the quiet (wind & the bell
clanging outside) only this restless streaming night, fresh
wind off the sea, is where he is. Water, candle changing in
the draft, turns slowly cool. Ripples when i lift my fingers
edge around this streaming, in the river-sea outside that winds
around our time, this city, his father's father ...
                                        'delivered'
is a coming into THIS stream. You start at the beginning
& it keeps on beginning.

Rings, iv.

Eyes shut. Relax now, can relax all over, breathe like
asleep, pretend to be sleeping if you can remember how it
feels, whole, your whole body, before it comes again. But
don't think of that now, relax. Al, listen, Al's still
reading,

> *'I beg your pardon, the doctor said. 'I am perhaps*
> *a little jealous since you use your language to communicate*
> *with yourself and not with us ...*
>> (can't get comfortable,
> To relax. Wrong side maybe.)
>> *'I do my art in both languages,'*
> *Deborah said, but she did not miss the threat ...*

>> (oh there's
the sheet, the, Beginning to tighten now, lie still, Relax
everything but that, now, A breathing, climb, higher, B,
breathe higher, C, it's all turning to, liquid, hot, spasm
(smother), OH, very deep in, all, in it grinding me to liquid
shit again ... shit.

> Up. Al: again? Can't help it. That damn
enema. And that i ASKED for it, thinking it would rid me of
this feeling, this, terrible urge to go, got to, hurry (totter)
down the hall in this, ridiculous, gown. I feel like a child
half out of clothes, bare back cool. To get there before (ah,
this long corridor almost normal, window, life goes on out
there's a busy day, traffic
> Here. The door & tiled floor under
my feet, won't turn on the light it's so small & stuffy in here.

Sit, thank god, but now (crack of light under the door) if only
it would all come out. But what if i had the baby in the toilet,
in the dark. If i could just curl up on the floor there's not
even enough room (bet they made it like this on purpose) maybe
it's a natural urge) just to curl up in the dark on my own (cats
do it) on my own i could be calm. Here it comes, relax (how
can i relax on the toilet? should be back in bed) why did i
come? You should have known there was nothing more. Stop thinking
of that now, too late, breathe, It's tighter, breathe higher,
Oh, hands against the walls, hang on, no, let go, go into it,
don't fight it (all doubled up) don't fall into the toilet.
LET GO. Oh, that was bad. Hardly breathed at all. 'Cause you
were scared. Scared of being alone when it happened, when
something happened. After all that about the dark. Better go
back before it comes again.

     Down the hall. There he is, the
doctor, such a small man, owl man, & so imperious. But he
does look worried. Where were you? Now don't get up again.
You're not supposed to be wandering around after the waters
break.

   Little girl being scolded. But he was actually
concerned. Al in that silly gown ushers me in. They couldn't
believe you'd gone to the bathroom. Nobody told me not to.
I know, but you don't have to go anymore, you can't possibly
HAVE anymore. But it FEELS like it.

       Nurse pops in. D̄o you
want some demerol? The doctor said you could have some. Like
it was a gift.
   No.

    Up on the bed again (up on the roof, might
as well be.) With a little help (getting weak? feeling
well worked, sweaty). Now, find the right position. Because,
is it? Yes, it's coming again. Relax, breathe. Good, i'll

do it this time, i'll ride over it. Breathe higher. Remember
to relax everything. That leg too. Higher, faster, But it's
bearing down, Harder, not the right position, it's going to,
suck me in, quick, think of what Al's reading.

*By the light of
my fire, Bird-one, Anterrabae said* (breathe) *see how carefully, how carefully* (higher) *they separate you from small
dangers* (pant) *: pins and matches and belts and shoelaces
and dirty looks.* (It's going.) *Will Ellis beat the naked
witness in a locked seclusion room?*
Where is that?
a third of the way through? I can't remember. Wonder how long
it's been. Seems a long time i've been turning, twisting, half
the sheets on the floor. There must be some way, some position.
What did the book say for back labour? Try it on your side,
face Al, the book, the sunny window. sunny. Now relax. It's
not pain, it crushes me, it grinds me into thick, hot, water.
it wears me down fighting it. If i could only, let go.

.   .   .

I've settled into it. Tired & floaty warm. Except my feet
are cold, Did they say that?   your feet will be cold. Al's
socks, & my legs all bristly, i didn't shave. Well it doesn't
matter, i can't get into that. Socks feel good.

Why couldn't i eat the soup? It smelled meaty, nourishing.
Chicken noodle. such work to eat the noodles. even the broth.
But the red jello they brought (& i spilled, sticky against
my leg), so cold & clear, sweet. like sun in Jim's wine glass
that time in nashville when the day stood still, all that
afternoon was dust in everything we ate, luminous, air

thick with it like pollen/ honey moved thru, always, never
notice. Coming, & it doesn't matter, i can ride it. be a
cat relaxed & lie so it contracts but doesn't move me,
stays, limbs dissociated while it, breathe higher, grinds
my belly, back, to liquid, panting's a familiar place
at work, it's going, it does work, the breathing does ...

'Well, really, every CASE like you ought to realize that
THAT HELL' — and she began to shake with shudders of high
shrill laughter — 'can't last any more than you can stand it.
It's like physical pain — tee-hee-hee — there's just so much
and then, no MORE.'

               It doesn't matter. He's right, or she is.
But i'm not the same as them, which seems so far away i can't
get into it. He is, though. I've never heard him read aloud
a drama, personalities. strange world. Strange book, but that's
all right, he's reading it to me. What was the book we were
going to? or the song we never did decide. Now it comes,
they said god save the queen if you want, higher now, i never
seem to need it, just climb higher, panting, feel it clench
deep, still the ends of me relax. panic's gone. Why didn't i
take demerol before?
               This could go on all afternoon, Al reading,
my warm sticky bed, sun thru the window, i know it's sunny
out there, afternoon, could go on for hours tho the hours lead
somewhere, lead me, i don't fight to get there. Is he really
into the book? I might tell him, but it doesn't matter,
let his voice move on. I feel warm & tired, catlike. Even
the blood trickling down is comfortable. it's me. it's
happening as if i KNEW how it would be.

Uuungh. Against the wall, push my arm against the wall &
push it thru my arm, that terrible urge to convulse, push,
get it out. No, it's a mistake, you're not ready yet, you
could hurt yourself. Don't push. I WANT TO twist my body
against it. want to constrict. Stay open, open. against
this WRINGING? It comes so fast, i've got to, got to. Don't.
And rigid, all my relaxation gone beyond it, hold the
pelvic floor loose & work it thru your arms,

                                         Uuungh, it's not
pain, it's got to, got to. that FORCE. I want to scream i
give up, twist into one tight fist, clench, & push it,
PUSH it.

      You're doing fine.

                        Ha. Why don't they let me?
You know why. Al, folding my arm & saying one two blow. He's
doing it too fast, but he remembered, he's doing it. Not yet.
Yet, yes, blow, blow. The book said you can't blow & push
at the same time. Blooow. You can. i still did. Don't.
Everything's speeding up. One, two, blowowow.

                               There's only a
little bit left, hang in there.

                 As if i can, as if i will it!
They don't know. Can't hang on much longer, going to, the
next one, going to give in. Oh now, blow. Try. You might
hurt his head. Blow. There's the sponge (Al) on my lips.
Can't open my eyes to thank him. Coming again. Ah, ah, can't
stop it, stop writhing around & pushing.

                       That did it,
the nurse said, that was the worst one, the others won't
be so bad.

And they're wheeling me out, it's happening. The open door.

. . .

A lot of people in gowns & they're all talking busy. A lot of white light. A table they slide me onto & there's the doctor, Well, smile. after all this we're ready! & the anaesthetist (? yes) & someone saying, Oh she's fine, she's doing very well. Can't answer. It's coming. Push. Again, push. Was i really pushing? It didn't seem to be pushing from inside.

And there's the mirror where i can see, except he's standing in the way. They've got me all positioned, knees up, feet in stirrups (fear, a bit). Al's at my head. There's so much going on i can't follow. so much talk. It's coming again, now push. Now someone's saying push. hard. that's still not hard enough. Going to have hemorrhoids tomorrow, all that blood rushing into my face.

I look up at Al behind the mask, his eyes look encouraging. Next time i'll be ready for it. & someone's saying, You can really push now, give it all you've got. I'm not doing it right. But it's so hard to tell when it begins & then it's here & i'm left behind, pushing, no. block & push. push. Too late, the tail end.

A shot? No, no, it's just salts. your blood pressure's high. Well at least i'm working, even if it doesn't feel right. But this time, this time i'm ready & remember, it's the blocking, build up pressure &, time it just right to (push), block &

PUSH ...

Nothing's different. There in the mirror hardly any hole, just
a little dark space. Why doesn't it change? How long has she
been listening to his heart with the stethoscope? Something's
wrong? Again now. Block &, push, PUSH. And the doctor's
saying, We're going to use forceps, he's posterior. What's
that again? face up? he's supposed to be face down? He's
lying relaxing with his hands behind his head, he says.
Relaxing?! Little person.

           And the anaesthetist is kind in
explaining what the epidural will do, what it will knock out.
The least, i say, i want the least. & the doctor: it's what's
best for the baby, he's getting tired. You don't have to
remind me, i want to say, i want him healthy, whole. of
course it's for him, whatever you say. & to the anaesthetist,
who is young & seems sympathetic, Will i still feel him?
You will feel something but you won't feel as much as you
would ordinarily, & you won't feel the epesiotomy. Yes, well
(that's not important). & they give it to me. & now he's
standing with Al drawing diagrams on my pillow of the nerves
which are getting knocked out. I can't feel the contraction,
the nurse has her hand at the top of my belly, she has to
tell me, now PUSH. & i push by sheer will because i can't
feel my muscles pushing down there, but i push. & it's a
good push. Someone said, there's a lock of dark hair. i keep
thinking, dark hair. Has he cut me yet? can i see? Whenever
i open my eyes the room is filled with white bustling,
everyone doing something specific. we're all working together
for him, for this one with his hands behind his head who
doesn't even know. When i look in the mirror it's much wider,
there IS hair. His hair! all matted against my red flesh.
Now lie back. & i feel the forceps go in, barely. There's
the head, they say. Now gently, now hardly push at all.
& i feel something like a loss, like the end of a sigh,

A cry! a squall of absolute protest, pain? He's real. &
i haven't seen him! & someone says a boy (i knew) with
black hair. They lay the cord on my stomach & he's upside
down, streaked with blood, & reddish, his small round buttocks
& head all wet, matted, all that hair. They turn him, such
big balls.

       He's crying. I can't stand it, i want to hold him,
PLEASE. & they lay him snuggled in a blanket on my stomach.
He's perfect, bawling, little blue fists. small & perfectly
HERE. He's here, i say to Al. & he's beautiful. Al's
bending over, a little shy but grinning too. & he is,
& i say to everybody, he's beautiful. Most of all to him,
because he's come thru that ring of flesh, into our light,
he's BORN, tight fisted in my arms, eyes screwed shut,
shutting us out. Yet he can hear & maybe feel someone
cradling him against her, hush. hush. i hold him. it's
all right. you're born.

Rings, u

Time to go in, from the afternoon grass, lifting him,
nudging the pram under shadow of the house. From after noon
sun keeps pouring, light we live in, thick with, smell of
grass fresh cut down the street, bird song, hour after hour
the cats, wary in long grass hunting elusive wings. His face
hardly tanned, eyes hurt in light, careful, turning with him
in my arms to keep his face dark

                              turning, wheeling with him in
my arms, hand up shadowing his eyes, from light, intensive sky
blue, into blue under, shell light over the radii of trees
reaching their upturned arms high overhead, my head, over
his, the cats' eyes filled, all, luminous cavity of brain,
with light:
                    this newborn (reborn) sensing, child i am with him,
with sight, all my senses clear, for the first time, since
i can remember, childlike spinning, dizzy...

What go-oes up, must co-ome down. Up the back steps, stagger,
hold him up lightly for my arms to absorb the shock to him
(springs) as once my water did. & into, shoulder against
the door, dark kitchen smell people have lived in, years
(old lady, all her windows nailed against the sun). Now,
door ajar for cats, it lightens, wind blows thru our curtains,
sun pours into the front room i see it, crossing the back,
shine along a length of wooden hall. His room's still faint
blue under the white, red curtains made so air moves specks of
colour, yellow, breathe.
                              And laying him down (my arms unroll, un-
burden) on the white sheet, he begins to kick, anticipating
diaper change, yes, wet. Unpinned now, folded on the can lid,
heat will condense in little drops by the time i get back &,

now his legs are waving free, he likes that, smiles, fists
waving too, slow motion under water dance us both, reeds, & the
dark at the back of my eyes ...

imminent dizziness from heat. from
light to dark. too dark. Concentrate: red buttocks: cream
(cold & white). big balls & penis & the fabric soft against them.
Folding in to pin, he doesn't like that, cries. Have i poked him?
No. Ever? Maybe natural fear of binding, or my apprehensive
fingers. Hi blue eyes, funny face so blue

as the sea, unknown.
What you see, when will you smile TO me? (believing already you
know who, in the hospital gaze at my hair, my mouth, & know my
voice.) But smile? They say it's gas fleeting, pucker. whimsy.
You know, little one. with smallest frown unfocused between
your brows. Hungry? Yes, it's time.

& light. Wind's blowing
the curtain, see, patterns of light like waves falling
across the floor. & cool now on my skin, unbuttoning
blouse, evaporates, my sweat from the sun gone. You?
cold? The cotton blanket, all your things, that delicate
smell you're wrapt in, new. But you must smell the
grass on me, sweat, insects, earth? These things you'll
spend hours with. All right, i'm hurrying. & the milk's
already dripping. That's your world. Hunger surge, mouth
open already crying. pain? There, into the rocking chair's
familiar fabric against my back, elbow up to support your
head, & nipple lifted towards. You're drinking now, those
hungry sucking movements of mouth, palate like little fish.
And snuggling down myself into the chairback can relax now,
So, The day is still,
　　　　Again,
　　　　　　This world. Something precious,
, something out of the course of time marked off by clocks.
Wind blows, plants breathe out their odours drawn by sun,

drifts, gradually over the house, shadows the back lane
lengthen, birds too, active at different times remark,
their wings worm's activity, the day's age ... daze, an
age was all i knew, child in blue sea dress & bare legs,
climbing from terrace to terrace. Uncalled (from home),
called, by the focus of an orchid, length of tree shadow,
sun a glint on sea below, the island light, passing from
mainland out, to sea, to see *where* time turns, known by
intensity of odours, orchids', & the earth here,

                                        Here's
lilacs outside your window. Lilac time i brought you home in.
Thick fragrance up the back lane our car drove thru, Al
drove thru, ecstacy, to be outdoors again, get out on grass,
springy, unlike cement or hospital floors my feet had known
a week, & you had never known it, smelt, the sun. in every
blade, leaf, culm. breathing light. & never known the
lilacs i'd thought old lady flowers a dying, virulent as
fever (ecstasy

           Cold at my heart *(must co-o-me down)*,
times you're so quiet (sleeping) when i bend can't tell if
you're breathing still. & Al: of course he is. The cats,
Conch in your crib the other day. by suffocation. sudden
death. Wake up suddenly past the hour you should have woken
cried for milk, Come running down the hall, fear at my throat,
The time, the time it takes to reach your door, open it,
draw near (slow motion, slow, reluctant) Find you sleeping
still.
      The fear.
                Stops. Up my heart, stops breath. Stop
the circle *(spinning thru, Drop, all you troubles by the
river, side, Catch a painted pony on the spinning wheel ride.)*
Which does spring on thru. It's fear of the unexpected, of
the music suddenly broken off. It's fear of it happening

104

When ... ? ('Is the music over, Mom?')

Let the spinning wheel spin.

                                    & the pressure
built p til it hurts in the other breast, is full, towel
tuc   d under wet, & you, long hard pulls now, almost empty,
ti e to shift you. Lift you up, little head on my shoulder,
stroke that burp that never comes between times, only after,
only they say, burp him between breasts, & i grow tired of
hurting, & you, maybe want some more, or maybe fall asleep,
already? I put you down in my arm, left side i never can
arrange it right, so your nose is free to breathe & your
head not turned in some way awkward as the other never is.
Left side, sinistra. But you're eager. No need to suck,
it's there, drip from the nipple, tho you do, must, i figure,
your gulping that swift, spurt, like a water fountain down
your throat.
          Connect. Open conduit, light or liquid flowing
thru. you. in the circle my arms make around you drinking
sun, my own, skin, hair absorbed, what you now take in. all
that you need.
          Tho it seemed so thin-looking when it first
came, in a milky water. all the nutrients are there. &
still it runs. more as you want more, grow more. Amazed,
at the interconnection still. Those first days how, with
every suck, i could feel the walls of uterus contract. You,
isolate now, & born, healing my body for me.

No wonder he grows strange, feeling so, outside. Never comes
in when he comes home, only sometimes, news to tell. But
usually (no news? bad news) heads into the kitchen or the
bathroom. Ritual of coming home. Jacket on chair (hot?)
sleeves rolled up, neck open (tired & edgy) heads for ice,
scotch. The end of a cement day of hospital floors. Walls.

Still there.

Walls & clocks he has to move by. Watch (face
of the sun) he never takes off, wound by the action of his
wrist each day a myriad gestures, tasks, the way he writes,
backhanded. Backwards (stubborn), moving back.

Last night's
dream sat up in the middle of the bed to hold him, catch him
falling thru a confusion of falling Kit was him. & only
woke him.

Fear

Stopt the wheel, the music falling out of
time. & *the painted pony*, Rides on up & down, riderless.
retreating.

The unborn.

Who-is-it? lives, a dark unknown.
No two feet on the ground, no gravity in water, no sense of
weight. His own, his own weight known to him.

My fear's then
not that you die who i've barely known, but not be born, Not
bear yourself alone & learning it, your birth into the light of
day, dazed, the risk we all take, pushed out into it.
No one a mother to you, no — the uterus itself contracts
& pushes its burden out. At a certain point (in time)
ripe as a fruit, a weight, the intimate night's expelled.
made light. made isolate one in the world,

the wheel. My
arms make around you spinning as the world does, we wheel thru
light & dark. One day's going (birds & wind, leaves tightening
as our warmth does) into night.

What can i tell you,
little one, that you don't already know? Nestled there
half asleep, yet sucking, dreamy, open to milk, to all you

want & all that afflicts you, hunger, gas, light, irritation.
Self contained there in my arms that weigh the burden of you.
Your small face. Knowing, Unknowing, i will bend over,
shade you plantlike as the sun turns, deepening toward
suppertime & the night, light outside your window cut
off by the house, by five o'clock.

Cars whirr by outside, gravel spews. (A certain motor.
Gears down, stops. News from outside coming home.

Rings, vi.

Your hands on the steering wheel. steer us. turning, new
corners of the moment, loops, curves back? having, you'd
underlined it, left behind that taint of city & our past. lives.
Return? No. It's new our going over the bridge, tonight, our car
finally fixed, bottle of wine bought over a week ago for this,
uncorkt (unstopt

      headway, you & i? & this one not yet sleepy,
smiling up at us in all ignorance even seducing our attention
from

   (not yours) highway, dusk worn away to, threads of light,
somewhere out there, over river & delta fields, the grown grass
summer tall, odd lamps of houses we flash by, unknown — you
keep your hands on the wheel, driving us into dark, your
profile taking long swallows now from the bottle, Well, back
of your hand across your mouth, that's it,

          we're out.

            (meaning,
an old amazement) meaning (your words wrenched to) you're excited,
or making yourself, us both so, making sense of our going, not
just one more trip. Is this, yes, you say, final, finally free.

Of what? your past i think, i never knew it's where you live, on
that edge: the border calls. call it nostalgia, not for home, for
open country/ film of america we saw, yellow buggy jouncing across
widescreen panavision's promise. & after, came out into the delta,
driving thru fields, into, under a row of trees unravelled, wind,
watched, both of us adolescent in short sleeves stirred by sun
more real than movie colours clear the fields of ocean horizon —
here, i said, is *our* 'country' — you agreed, fading

         on our mantel
this past year to coloured bits in lights, your brighter dream:

blue mailbox house in the country, nashville, going down the
backroads, We are going, back

                       into/ Life-size colour, that fable,
that it's new, a different place for us to make our lives in, new
now. Come back. kiss. little one, almost asleep. & i'm too
comfortable at this hour, twilight lengthening, to shift him
to the back, to bed, from where he dozes deep in our closeness ...

How do you feel about leaving? (for good) That question (if it
is good. if we can make it so.) Hard to realize, i mean it
doesn't seem ... (inarticulate, not saying there are walls
(& gates, doors ...

            There's always holidays or perhaps a summer
on one of the islands, you say (not what you intend? or what i
think you admit, as possibility?) Surface of cement speeds by.
A positive charge, an obvious forward-looking. Energy. Means
your different take on this thread spinning out before us, spinning
back where i am holding, as you drive us out beyond the city
limits

      ... as if that fucking town was trying to hold us back, you
say, when the car failed, i never thought we'd make it.

                              Only,
how much is "it" a half dark place, light winding far down
horizon now, lower fork of river surface we slide under – to,
just catch the outline of moored ferry, Tunnel, before its
underpass rushes to engulf us, barelight concrete holding
off the force of river pressing down above, muffled, might
at any instant bury us in its present ... We rush thru where
day/night makes no difference.

                  Is he asleep yet? Not yet.
Why don't you put him down, perhaps he will then. (Meaning,
you want my undivided presence.) So, turning to kneel on the
seat, arms extended lay him down carefully in the rising bed.

There (his small dark head, eyes open now, smiles at my smile)
sleepy? There's Doggy (crook of his arm, ridiculous plastic
ears & glued-on wink he recognizes, special sound in his
throat, as

       (aah, the wine, back of his father's hand dropping
down)

       Is there pleasure? Son smiles. Father ... ? Sun,
low down if not gone already, dusk, aura of smile traced in
eyes face half obscured.

              Faced with this driving you do, lulled
i sit, we both sit. constantly ahead of ourselves, & feel this
cleaving. dark. which once, you said, was cleaving a clinging
to? (she cleaves to him) or splitting as ships cleave sea or —
night, two ships that pass etc (ship lamp), dark

                          our car splits,
carrying us forward into it, yet always where we are, lit, warm,
full of the known/ Unknown thoughts sift between your ears, sift
in the silence of our passing. How do you feel? Knowing, as you
do say it, Good. Meaning absolute.

              It's hard to believe ... Yes,
that this is it. (to make sure you state it, up against the wall
We're leaving. no way back.) But. What? I say it as if for the
city, We didn't really get into it this time. You didn't. (Me?
on whose terms?)

       Lilac, Is lilac all there is? That backlane
not yet oiled for summer, heavy with it, four trees, three corners
of the lot, & other backyards, dusty gravel past, brokedown cars &
ancient coal bin, flats in the distant streaming, Fraser, Bob's
house, streets over, shaded by the tree & night, Rory's (music?)
raided, over all their gnarled trunks even in abandoned lots a flood
of fragrance ... SPRING'S ... renewed matter grows, it matters, these
mutterings ...

as, flip, you say: What was there to get into?
it's changed, it's not the same city. That was. & is. No other
than what it was that we grew up in. (i have no defense.) Convinced,
you say it's nowhere, nothing's happening for us in it. Its
avenues extend, under coldflame, empty. even now, weeknight down
suburban streets parked cars & deadeye stores blink slow &
downtown pubs are burning, no one, only, half there looking for
familiar chairs & table, empty, stares at pallid still life, some-
time vague desire, cut off, shuffling, one foot in front of the
other, a step, in the right direction ...

                                         What're you so
quiet about? Dunno (how *say* it?), the road's, hypnotic in the
dark ... Not much traffic tho. How can you keep your eyes open
when the lights pass? (mine range invisible country while you
keep yours on the road & headlights) Don't you? They're too
bright. It just takes adaptation. Ah, breathing in the dark ...

Here. You hand me, unquestioning gesture, wine. Tastes so
WHAT is it? Oh Eschenauer Saint something. Soon we'll hit
the california wines, drinking, hot in / soft green light from
radio barely, huge curlicue, the E, Saint-Julien. softer than
dry california taste going down (its edge to lean on, like The
Bridge, Aug 3 crossed out. You showed me. For Oak St Bridge
Aug 3 crossed to 7 '69. I understood, saw you bent over in your
intent lettering (curve of back & to be hugged aloneness printing
'goodbye city' ...
                  What is Vancouver but dark shadow
port its aura, its bright doorway, empty as any other strung from
mountain smallness of us two bodyclose back to forest staring at
the promise laid at our feet (we thought), city of phosphor, ours,
our (false) unreadable map — we have diverged from,
                                     you: goodbye
rotten city, having come a long way thru closed doors. No. this

city rings us, rings its harbour's dark water, dark heart of the
lights we live, part of our skin, dying as it is, our past, tho we
emerge from it,

                    Drawn along the highway of lights
illuminating what our two heads move in, green glow of dials &
levers, restful base hum, & the smell of wine spilt, drying in
the heat our bodies make (i need it), in cigarette smoke, in our
shared aura (is it?) ...

We're at the border. Yes. Were you falling asleep? No. Just
musing in the dark, the moving ... You'd better hide the wine, roll
down your window so he doesn't smell it.
                                     I need a cigarette.
Here. & the lighter. Use the car's. Oh yes (forgot, not often
smoking, don't register each time he uses it, the times, lost in
my own place to be.)

                    We drive straight thru, around, the
Canadian (no one visible) inspection house, & down toward the
American. Car stopped ahead in the line we choose. Customs
officer looks somehow less official, more bored? not unkind but
overly curious in a way, leaning on the sill of the car, his
manner recognizably (small shock) American. What we're re-
entering.
        Do you have Kit's card? So new it doesn't even bear
his photograph.
        In my hands on my lap the cigarette smokes.
I don't want it now. While you, lighting one, pull on it hard,
bright, it flares. We move up in the line to the man asking us,
Where are you going? For how long? We tell him, record of our
crossing the cards in his hand, Immigrating. Do you have
anything else in the car besides household goods? (A child.)
No, you flick the cigarette against the metal edge of the tray.

Okay, he says. We're out.

                         Past the Peace Arch, muck flats of
Blaine, Or in, America. Its neon signs flickering thru our
past, its main street full of taverns we know, Wagon Wheel, the
liquor store, road house, all, the nights we drove back,

Forward now. On new ground, you say, your profile to me, non-
committal, both our heads unknown to eyes in the back seat asleep
in the wheels' moving still burning point of my cigarette its
ash ring outer skin of flame, our turning, words

                                   their point,
continuing to spin in mind. Are we out, as you said? This trip,
this time. A brilliant highway heralded by arc lamps overhead
that turn, in the wind of our passing into, dark.

he was born Saturday afternoon May 3rd at 7 minutes to 5 of a sunny day.

have since found out he was a forceps delivery all the way — extracted, like a
tooth. I didn't push him out. also that I had torn close to the sphincter, a
hook "like a hockey stick," Ross said. they stitched me up. so high I was
hardly aware.

he is lovely. I worry about him. when he sneezes, when he hiccups, but am
making myself enjoy each day. the last 2 mornings sun has come in on the
bed when he's feeding. at 10:00 he was so sleepy I had to make him work to
suck, tickle his bare feet. then he fell asleep in the sun against my breast.

but he's separate already — pushed my hands away with his. & if he doesn't
want to suck he simply refuses to take hold. trying to focus, sometimes a
worried expression like 'what are you *doing?*' stares at my hair often, & my
mouth (most moveable part of my face.) probably sees only a small part of
my face but may recognize my voice, seems to be listening. really so
self-*contained,* such a total little entity tho he *is* dependent on others for
survival.

May 12/69

yesterday, Mother's Day, came home with Kit (that seems to be my name
for him). in a week all the trees out fully leafed (arch of young pale leaves
like butterfly wings along Blenheim). along King Edward the cherry petals
were falling, circles of pink light under each tree. & down the back lane,
home, the lilac out. Al driving slow as much for the $100 of liquor in the
trunk for his alcohol experiment begun today.

& back into the world. Bob & Donna with DR came round. we opened the bottle of champagne Eric had brought. Bob grave, suffering hangover from Rick's wedding previous night. Donna holding Kit, nostalgic. Vera making friends with DR. Al & Bob talk, but also Al looks over at me sometimes, special look. I'm mostly dazed, suffering shock from contrast of dimensions — after one room in the hospital, the house looks huge, airy, gleaming clean (thanks to Vera). how did I ever manage this place, cooking, cleaning, & being with Al & now Kit? panic. so used to the rigid system of the hospital which supported me, ways of caring for him passed on to me from the nursery, had got the rhythm down well in my own room, now everything's different, not only different things to work with but different space to move in. after first feeding/changing him I got uptight. nothing's where I can find it or ready, a series of minor crises. horrified later, phoning Donna about diaper pail, to learn dirty diapers must be rinsed by hand in toilet. Kit's grumbling, crying — almost time to feed him again.

later

I understand Donna's post-partum blues as she explained it, "I didn't feel good enough for him." for me it is different — I felt reborn with him, that clear, pure feeling, childlike, & in my emotions I was. started to cry when Ross said he thought maybe I should go home Monday not Sunday. tears always close to the surface, either from terrible feeling of aloneness & responsibility, or simply because my stitches hurt so much — to crying from pure joy, especially at nursing times, just holding him, his head with all its dark hair against my skin. a feeling of wonder, & often a tremendous sympathy with *his* tears, his hunger or miserableness.

days of such blinding light I will not forget: mornings in the bathroom, sun streaming thru the window, clean white towels everywhere, white tile, a steamy warmth from the last woman's bath & from big silver radiator the towels were set on. & as I undressed, steam rising from ready water, the milk would be dripping from my breasts onto the floor. or lying in bed feeding him, naked from waist up, Kit sucking at one breast while milk trickled from the other down my body. never felt so plentiful, never been so delighted with my body, that it was more than adequate. me, the skinny teenager who never seemed to become quite a woman.

May 16/69

two weeks ago today he was still in my womb. strange to think of all that hair in there. he's grown more than to fit back inside. noticed yesterday he seems to have discovered the feel of his legs — anyway kicking & stretching them, not always curled in uterine position. long legs. almost kicked over the basin of water while being changed.

such anxiety: in tears today because I knelt on a rusty nail — sure I'd get tetanus, transmit to him thru my milk (*could* it happen?) it's the strain of feeling so much miraculous.

world thru his eyes? only a haze Warren says. does he know when he's outdoors? knows my breast even under clothes — rocking him to stop his crying tonight he turned toward it open-mouthed. looking at him after nursing sometimes feel he's still lost in another world, that fleeting secretive gas smile, as if smiling at his own thoughts — all turned inwards.

digestive functions such a large part of his awareness & preoccupation — stops sucking to shit & the shit seems almost to explode out of him — he can't do both at once. often when I sit him up to burp he lets out little groaning sounds, the bubble just sitting in his system. squalling: arms, legs, head all going at once — general distress. feel him very much at the mercy of, not only helpless in face of outside threat but also helpless before the internal.

"Christopher": figure of secrecy, of unknown,— travelling from it. figure of inward. deep in some secret enjoyment (pleasure is secretive only in that it's not accessible to others who can only guess its feel)

communication: the central problem of Rings.

rings: bubbles: coffee perking, Kit to be burped (bubbled) — little white liquid bubbles between his lips & that bubble that must be stroked up from his stomach

rings: Bob's retold stories — trying to communicate a feeling, framed in story (anecdote) — need to be with people, that social ring

drinking: milk/beer: that closeness

May 25/69

you've got a debt to pay   (I don't care how rich you are)
you've got to go back to mother earth

mother — death as much as life — source of mother fear — natural realization of a taking for every giving — double-handed mother

May 30/69

wondering in letter today if fear of Kit's dying, of losing him, is due to increased sense of death's presence in life, as of silence behind sound. life such *activity* now, such a slender miracle in face of it. because I was present at his coming into it as a separate one, a journeyer.

every Saturday I celebrate to myself that he's lived another week & lived it strongly. that he gains his own defences: his voice louder now, can move his head more freely, kick & thresh his arms.

that I "gave him life" as they say, but was powerless doing it – more like my body only the means for his coming into his own life. me totally subject to that event. so if life itself is so much not our initiative, death even more so. or not quite that. there *is* the sense of making our own lives, that life is our effort to live, fully, as against the blank of death. so what I see is the *effort* for his small body, small resources – & yet delight in the vitality, his rolling around, his infantile pugnaciousness, his protests.

July 18/69

talk with Al: fear of Kit's dying connected somehow with fear of our relationship dying. or a displacement onto him from the absence between us.

he warns me against becoming as overprotective as he sees his own mother. repeating patterns (rings) to be caught in. this is his analysis but it chokes up the openness of my loving.

does everything go awry when he stands awry in his work? is this the basic mis-step? "a mistake" he called our coming here.

so we leave at the end of the month. out of all this detritus to make it shoot up new again, our life together – in a house in the country near Madison, just as he imagined. the photo came in the mail today & it does look good. a tobacco farm. my imagination stops at the edge of the page.

Wisconsin

Old Stage Road
Brooklyn, Wisconsin

tobacco shed only other
building in view

fields & fields & sky

cloudy morning
wind:
            invisible sea, moves like one, always at the edge of consciousness,
                    rolling in from the edge of earth —

first Vancouver poem written here — feelings sorted/realized to some extent

thinking on grass outside, Kit & I the only people in all this space (Al's
1st day of classes in Madison): it's the work that gives me the right to
                    speak,
                        to matter, only so far as the work —

                    coming closer to understanding Duncan's
                    sense of being *in the service of* (poetry, lan-
                    guage)

a straining after worth, significance in the writing — "the right to speak" (be
"worthy"? of being heard) is only a reflection of its inverse, a feeling of
worthlessness, a personal dis-ease
                        that it doesn't matter how childish I am
to myself, or that Al sees me as a child either because he needs to or because
that is what I show him — fearful childish fears of facing the world, revealing
self inadequate, brought out by opportunity of this poetry circuit thing —
fears of not "measuring up" — to what measure? only what I see of others'
abilities?
            in short, it's not who I am that counts but what I can offer — of

work, of care. felt I never had the right to speak out as a social member because I didn't belong — cut off in part by myself because I rejected the values of those around me — but then discovered a community of writers whose values helped me recognize mine — enlarged again to the possibility of a renewed society I want to be a part of

in the Vancouver poems, the city's dream of the city, underlying what is.

October 22/69

ERO: Earth Read-Out (Berkeley): "the Unanimous Declaration of Independence"

MAKES SENSE! in terms of where to go, what direction. so busy being here I forget time's moving on. (or is it? maybe only moving back on itself — the planet does. yet we grow old.)

Ads on TV — happiness voice of wife or husband, for house deodorant or new detergent: frightening thought that perhaps there *are* families like that — not just made up by ad-men but a true reflection of the "norm"?

thinking yesterday, my day in town (Madison), anxiety level high may be so for others besides me & the "apathy" of city people re accidents, crime, is wrongly diagnosed. more like such acute over-reaching ("driven" by time, by traffic, by abstract obligations) that each ends up helpless on a treadmill of own making — can't get off on any side, break the routine or let it by broken by the untoward. city of walking mummies, all driven by demand: drive "right," work "right," live "right," because if you don't you upset the system, "others are depending on you."

the refeshing waywardness, refusal to participate in systems (the orneri-ness) of skid row drunks, bums, drop-outs of all kinds. so the Vancouver poems centre partly on them.

                       rings of them, camping out on the streets.
they link up with each other in random arrangements. the ecological movement of words, the way they link up in several directions at once. "casting a
backward reflection." RINGS of influence. to break the notion of forward
progression — progress in the name of which DDT, atom bomb, nuclear
power.

most stimulating direction in ERO program of four changes: "more research
into non-polluting energy sources; solar energy; the tides": making use of
what's at hand, what surrounds, instead of imposing our inventive/
destructive project on the planet. the vision of Atlantis, of a race of graceful
knowledgeable beings in harmony with their environment & cosmos, tides
of energy washing in & out of person as of planet & universe.

                                           January 29/70

New Year's Gang & fire bombings in Madison — hard to take uncalled for
destruction — not the old gym so much as what it contained: office of
graduate students' organization for water purification, office for Indian
students (1 boy lost all his stuff) — "accidental" victims. no regard for life of
the Munitions Plant employees in Baraboo, also bombed — even tho they're
morally wrong to be employed there

                               but still who are those people doing the
bombing? if they aren't just "speed-freaks" — if they're people who are fed
up with offering themselves as martyrs to cop brutality in peaceful demos?

Al says they're turning the public against their very project, you can't
change people's minds by violence. so you tell them they've got to go on
prostrating themselves for hard knocks in order to protest? — like the
welfare marchers & the way they were set upon. Al says things do

ultimately change, witness last week's Supreme Court decision about not punishing draft dissenters by changing their status.

in any case the state will ultimately crush this small a number of violent revolutionaries. but the unknown factor is their anger (Milwaukee White Panthers in Village Church last Friday) & their waiting, after so many knocks. as Marv says, they've got to take a stand somewhere, even if it does lead to people & property getting damaged. it's the Black Panther virility issue: you can't be a man when you're being victimized so you fight back.

February 16/70

Clayton (Eshleman): poets work to make the sun come up (& I think of *Black Orpheus*)

if so, it's not a matter of pretending to divinity but
        2 little boys playing & singing the sun up
        writing a daily part of life & as essential
        that the sun come up for me, in me, as for those kids

in the sane light of day I think that to *realize* our life is the same as to write

& there is this sense of gaining ground in understanding
(increments of
        as amounts of daylight seasonally

& equally I lose some of what I know in dark periods

I have to remember the way — perception, in language — the transmission in language *of* language — *understanding* what's there
        "to stand under or among,
        hence, to comprehend"

what is "world" — space to move in
               EXTENT — limits of vision
               what one can *encompass*

— to encompass as much as possible (not narrow-minded
                                    no refusal — out of stubbornness or
                                    trying to exist at expense of others
                                    not exclusive — ramrod

dance from place to place (bee
     ecosystem: grassworld
or sail from cove to cove: mutual needs — take on water, fresh vegetables
                                  take away knowledge of place
                              — give? (not disease)
                              should be exchange, products/knowledge

Columbus setting out in his vision — honorable & maximum use of 'man' —
but ends up colonialist plundering

it goes wrong where actual contact occurs: he could only see distances & not
the close-up, at hand, what was to be toucht not taken
     failure to *meet* the other (persons, objects)

power corrupts & power desired for freedom (*em*powered) especially to overrule,
                                    empire — enslaving others

but, interrelations, exchange is *shared* power (energy commune process)

"world" is social as opposed to "earth" since man is the basis — (basest?) —
measured by time by which he measures himself, hence the (rat) "race"

limits of vision / limits of comprehension: THAT THE OTHER EXISTS the other side of the ocean or earth, dark side of the moon

EACH MOVE MADE HERE (me) MOVES THERE (you)

February 23/70

worold "age of man"   "course of man's life"

— that Columbus saw beyond the horizon (limit) "the other side of the world" envisioning a whole few others could, at that time, in the patchwork world of 15th c. Europe. a global sense of — you go around it (not off the edge) & the outer limits (ends) connect, no edge

but what is "the world out there" as if existing apart from us? there's "a world in a grain of sand." world is shared & communicable — world is what human creates out of earth. "a whole world" in a lifetime — "the whole world's there" (here, make it here)

March 16/70

ring of owls yesterday, Kit in my arms, near dusk, we walked into their calling — from the western edge of the farm, pines beyond pond, to pines beside & back of house, calling to each other — us stalking, so close all pitch vibrations rung in ear but unseen — voices of the far-off brought in close & almost tangible

Duncan's "an owl is an only bird of poetry"

writing to Larry: "there is only the one immediate, personal salvation, of
the psyche, your own, without help since help is maternal/paternal & that is
the very caul that must be thrown off. to be born: to MATTER ..."

made matter: the issue: what matters: issuing thru the ring of the invisible
to ground — or hearing: as the vowel carries breath to make a sound

&

sounding, thru the ring of surrounding phonemes, it changes — hearing
change the very matter of

Columbus Poems

in Spanish,
Cristoval Colon;

in Italian,
Cristoforo Colombo,
which is his real
name

colours

brown
grass green
may,

a little head,

Colombo wait —

blue eyes out
stare

    this world

greens in
my eyes, his
on the brown there

at ease

& satiate, you
smile up at
what cue what
response?

my slackening of arms'
tense
     now
necessity's gone

"island of Guanahani"

your finger flower
motile in air
unclose
      after
           hard
sail
   (night
from Europe's close

this shore means
light, What sways in
drinks in

        (all manner of eye

things too seem to be
watching you

crib bars, birds
(their sky grasp
air
   flowers feel

do move in
vision'd now

Columbus will

turtle neck strain
eyes cry see
for dream's sake

    (remarks, a
      moony head

somebody up there
doesn't like me, late
face again
            (how
              human to be
              hands out
              wanting smiles

around the deck

no Noah's flop of
comedy's respect

      (a hope
      a 'seen' a

      moon —

hands feet do kick out
(anger at

small turtle hates
being overturned

turtle for name
"Tommy" we gave
sight, sound, smell etc
how we know, or you
                    WHO
                    "can you
                    hear me?

Cid, the split
knowing & feeling
    "doesn't know he
only wants to sleep"
doubts
        you cry for the
        world at times over
        much

            want

no ears to hear
my tiptoe, wake
at the smallest
who-comes, clair
audient
        Taurus
                mix-up of
                animal i
                dentity, these
                creatures we
                 live with
                mobile of
                moo
                    graar
                        the blue

hooves or shell crystalline

tortoise before the
new world brought
turtle up
            a long
                        trip to
reiterate

            the unseen
            things we live with
                (Indies possibly

to sleep, turtle, dream
your patchwork shell of
memories at 6 months you
anticipate
                (imminent
                'boo' yet

                the sea creeps up unknown

see, you
sleep

sky lullaby

"3
men in a tub"
come
stopping his cry

    windy
        odour of
        up from
        no teeth to
        brush, gum
        semi
        transparent

exotica just this
unknown

        sun, dull, lit
        grass
        summer's end
        shone
            momen
            tarily con
            trary to
            environs

                      come

singing or crying
3 men do
in light of gum arabic or gum
of some instinctive
westerly

passage, Pizarro
blood run sea
swell engirdle

Cortez, a short
lived man

Columbus
in deference to
environs hung
the pull of re
lationship
           to moon
                        (now trash

"fishing for" I sung him
"stars," the 3
mythopoeiac
travellers of
sky a sea we

      live in
      nor can escape

parkt
by cedar
boughs the wind
      (to)
his crying un
seen
      ripple
            Chris
            topher Magellan o
            cean I
            swung you in

trans - it

Co
　　lum
bus at
sea ships
word
　　　alien
element as yet

do you drown?

dada
keeps self here
a voice
　　　　for company
mid ship
water creaking

given impetus (the word
will get you there

now merely
a sea of sound

look out

I worry
cold, does he
crowing, half
distress, half
exercise

Columbus
on the lookout see

    birds wheeling
    wing meaning

new way to
solace
    /one

finger to
the wind

protest

cool-
    aid for
Christopher's
not to be tossed
away, a sup
lost

my will to
make well

    DRINK THIS

crash of hand
fever heads
no captain keeled
in/
    subordinate

the breaking
edge of wave cool
claritas

"you cannot make him drink"

nor teach light
of its own arise

or make the sun come up?

pacing impatient his
bubble's breath to

break

    lost sun light hill

       HORIZON

merely, mere sea, offer
cool cool wave to
rest upon

"When I was young
I too went
sailing"

      & the kites
      day-glow in the
      window of
      seven-eleven

        but you
      recognize people as too
        (legged or like
      little of air
      currents

      running as yet
      unknown, caught

           in the flowerbeds
           my dress all
           tumble green
              in the Indies
              other side of
              instructed limit

      outrunning yourself run
      further than you think

      end up on a new
      continent concerned with
      paradise
           unfriendly
      snake-in-the-grass

& the sails droop

know, funny
bendy legs all
eager to
outstep
hands held, you

    sail, out
    sail the wind, run
    where the winds run

       there
          you

go

for Kit, your

chuckle, it
breaks at
larynx, a
bubble
  ticklish
  response upon

    (leaf rustle

you chuckle
like some windy tree
air current
breaks up thru

you 'break up'
seeping whole into
'the world'

    out where the inner
    man begins
    on edge

   a laugh
   sometimes provoked

irritable
leaf mimosa curling
water
  salts your
    laughter
    close to tears
      streaming

downstream leaf floats
minute boat calling
at the bank where current
holds some respite
        we say dallying

        the world of
        stream, rock, reed

        wind blows, boat
        calls
        into & out of
        small boy world
        we do not know

what you find funny, near
hysteria, the tree
that thru you streams
    its face calling
now you see me, see

        how does it look
        to you? the trees

rustle, sing, & not
wind which
rustles leaves
its trace only
evident as ash
of fire?

        "The ash
        is the tree of sea-

power ... of power
resident in water"

                    strangling other roots
                    little Woden, Wotan

rides thru time beats
thru the future
                bearing
in your root will ancient
tree of the world

against its end

            Woden ride
            the Night
            mare
                    Columbus astride
            unknown sea to
            the edge

                    this point ticklish
                    this bubbling hysteric
                        source

                            this well-
                being

wind blows, wind
calls
        one

particular leaf, you

run downstream to meet
my leaf, life

we also

touch

watching re-run Johnny Cash show tonight, Al spoke of story-songs,
American myths he said, both Cash & Marty Robbins sing — the outlaw
shot in El Paso, outlawed by love. (too easy to blame love, its failure, for a
prior condition.)

            but Cash's empathy with the outlawed, the imprisoned —
his convict's focus in railroad scene tonight, & the "Trail of Tears" of the
Cherokee, a reaching-out for the experience of these people, to express it.

ex-pression, not just self-expression, it's the pressure of feeling — throat as a
filter. Lorca, how he was a great singer, insofar as he expressed the feelings
of his people — not the nation so much as the Andalusians, a group. "your
people" are the people you feel kinship with, are inspired by even, moving
into a larger sense of "self" where a common feeling burns, moving to share
it, show it, through whatever medium — thought of fado & flamenco &
Lorca's piece on the singer. maybe genuine singing occurs when a large
experience (of a people) is forced through a small exit, the individual's
throat, "tongue", way of speaking.

or maybe the artist is always the one outside, yearning to belong. creates
what s/he wants to be a part of, makes it so, momentarily, in the art.

June 11/70

Eigner's work at location: inner/outer at once: event or presence (often
presence as event, birdflight etc) & the wondering about it (estimating
distance or time, or speculation as to elsewhere) work together in an I (or
eye, simply, perception) that locates itself by what surrounds it. a most
accurate report of being in the world.

so much of what gets written speaks only of the social (exclusively human) sphere, for which the earth we walk (that "supports" us) is merely an old-fashioned backdrop, or else a symbol & generalized. as if one's presence at any given moment isn't much of how air feels on one's skin, wind or not, or heat, or cold, or what is underfoot, cement or grass etc. not just following the track of meaning, not just ideas & glances, pointed conversation. what about non-meaning, & who is me but a complex of other (objects & object-events) & maybe a little bit of memory, or speculation, or a little wanting.

getting away from the (capital) "I" Freud attempted to clarify, as if that would illuminate the dark surrounding — not by domination certainly, & locate the "you" in its temporal network of relation, *by* its. one good poem.

> LE   "the local
>   is   sub+tela (*web*)
>   the subtle bird"

June 24/70

> the mythic arises out of the thing looked
> carefully at, watched — hear its song —
> & cannot be divorced from that — as each
> thing has its shadow

Rothenberg quotes Eliade, *Shamanism:* "For the shaman-poet like the sick man ... is projected onto a vital plane that shows him the fundamental data of human existence, that is, solitude, danger, hostility of the surrounding world. But the primitive magician, the medicine man, or the shaman, is not only a sick man; he is, above all, a sick man who has been cured, who has succeeded in curing himself.'

when I worry about the narrative of the Vancouver poems I worry about the problem of ending when there is no story – how to sequence the poems so the personal moves into the public? & where will it end?

not a problem: the image for it is widening rings (water) that disappear on the outer edge *into* the city –

                                  where the I/narrator gives way to the "you" is not only Al (tho thru him I first got to know the city –

                                      here's the inverse for a woman poet of the man finding earth/cosmos etc in his woman (Kelly). so I saw the world in Al or he showed it to me – coming out, as I did, of practical convent of my childhood, isolation up Penang Hill, & then as immigrant, plus something of a puritan, certainly virginal & protestant work ethic all thru school – it was the *world* he brought me into, the hub of the city, interaction, the night lights (we were always going to "look at"), the hive –

can I address the "you" now of city?

151

July 4/70
Vancouver

it isn't just that they had the car accident & I wanted to come home to be
with them — it's that I also wanted to come home to this landscape, that Kit
should come to know his birthplace.

went down to Horseshoe Bay for groceries with Dad this morning. something about this place so restful to me my body relaxes into it — the
mountains, sea wind, small shops — from grandiose height of peaks to white
ferryboats crawling across blue sea, to post office where they know him, all
small, all nestled at the foot of the bay. here the scale is different — perhaps
because nature overshadows the people ("nature" — sounds so passive,
pastoral for this upthrust rock — just looked it up: from L. *natus*, born. *here*
again.)

space to be — not simply laid back or politically apathetic as Canada is always
described in relation to the pressure pot of the States — or not *only* that tho
that's so too: no large demonstrations against the war, no race riots, no mass
movements. the struggle is not open here but repressed, individual, hidden.
death hides around the bend in the freeway as anywhere in America, but
people don't talk about it, just as they don't talk about the war. it's not "our"
war, & yet we contribute to it, watching from the sidelines, standing on the
edge. Al likes being where the action is, & yet we only watch there too. I
never feel located as I do here. it's physical as much as anything — familiar:

the softness of air on skin, breeze, sails, wake of speedboat. it's sea water
shimmering around the rocks, the smell of arbutus & cedar, the richness of
earth — felt, seen — wellbeing — a well (of) being

Jane just phoned to say her father remembers there *was* a jack-knife span in the Second Narrows bridge, but it had been built over a shallow portion of the channel & wasn't effective so in the 40's they built the elevator span. so the poem was right.

the writing is after something at bottom wordless, a complex in time where imagination/memory click with environment. each day of writing much like one cast of a net. the cast may come up with only a small piece of the whole or nothing at all. I criticize my net on the basis of its cohesiveness, its knots & how they generate each other. but each rewrite is also a re-cast. "It" is so subtle, the fish, its quick-ness, may get completely away, leaving not even a memory of its shape,leaving me with only the net.

August 4/70

to understand the interrelating of bodies / words

KWAKIUTL: we live by the world = according as the world gives
(a hunter's, a gatherer's sensibility)

ecology of language: each word what those around it relate of it as it relates (to) them
"context"
(text, the weave, the net)

why these poems run on like prose — the ongoing line gives a larger context while the short lines tend to stress the words in isolation (Stein's nouns)

August 10/70

Glady asks why nothing about strikes when this is a strike-bound city? says
history of Vancouver is one of constant ripoff, from CPR on. what big
business uses up.

not writing a history of the city. want to let the city speak *thru* the poems, its
things, its persons. not trying for breadth, scope (cover the *whole* city —
can't) but depth (uncover), cut thru different time strata at once.

sh'te the figure of: out of the sewer (offal, what's left after 'use')

> value in the "rubbish" as in the rubbies, living visibly
> on an edge we all live on

around & underneath the concrete, a sea of spirits moving — 1st human
recognitions of the place, Kwakiutl, Salish

September 9/70
Wisconsin

back again, we keep trying to make it work again — as if hope were a small
spark of the past we keep alight — alive in Kit.

i'm here & not here.

just realized — writing to Warren, the gratitude I felt on rereading his letter
— my need to *commune*, his word. not just the telling but the being
together, it springs up there. it wasn't only being close to Bob, but also
Warren, the city & all the others (the party, the Alcazar, the night at Glady
& Cliff's) —

& thinking for some reason of Clayton's criticism, "awash" he said, realize I need to be in those currents of Vancouver (crablike), to feel the wash, be entered by them — the larger currents out there.

afraid to be isolated on the farm again.

October 8/70

driving down alone in the red volvo, Kit in the back seat asleep, dusk, sun tipping all the grasses & prairie in the Arboretum a rose-gold hue — after the department picnic Sunday. thinking of energy, of the good feeling that drive gave me, & now, down 94, almost dark, hills rolling away from either side of highway, lights on in isolated farm houses, old horse in a field, chewing — & sense of animals asleep in the zoo or still — & what all the small creatures around us, unseen, in the trees are doing. my balanced frame of mind, my ease, thanks to balance again, finding my place, suddenly realized came from larger context of what was happening all around me.

my energy
(potential output) directly equal to the intake, the energy of the day I'd tuned into —

no Martian (Spicer) writing the poem, tho it is in some sense other (not-me), but energy of the whole stream — sensual in that way as anything alive picks up sensation, reading it — the larger wave we live in

October 10/70

at John & Kathy's — looking at Al:

>   my alienation is
>   screwing up our communication channels
>   static on the radio waves

December 12/70

today decided to leave. I am so tired of fighting to preserve some sense of who I am.

a little each day — write, to get back to myself.

all the anxieties about depriving Kit of his father, about the future, don't outweigh my need to survive. cold everywhere. the frozen lake, the locked car, keys dangling inside, the cutting wind — all metaphors for our state.

have to get back to Vancouver. step into the stream of my life there. find my own ground.

note

impatient, i
want to say
after Zukofsky's

    "rush ruins
      the whole hog," want

all of it held
at one
take

    old camera, that
    panorama, how?
    the eye travels

pierced
    /piece it to-
      gether, gather as
John said
at one shot en-
large the
horizon

    not

Mohican trail but
thru woods the
delicate hair fern under
foot pebbles
water bares

at back
up to three
thousand foot level

all words at
once that
relate
　　"If human life were a mountain or a flower
　　It could love itself — "

"mostly sand"

does VIADUCT
Georgia Street our past
bridge to Main make

    a bond?

transcend our coming in &
going, daily
        ties cut?

i'm all bridge
today, even rail
road we somehow
more than leaving indicates
both love

        torn down in
        memory a
        sequence of
        dead nights

severed
since going, shaky, is
speedup only
15 miles i said
it will collapse, but you
they made them solid in
those days

viaduct or way

across
      leading maybe
to a concourse we believe
extant, via this
decrepit

    bridge

ticktack

alder
        (heart
on the
wing, one
larch
        yellow
        reason raining

in my
sings all day blue
ticker ...

does the cat
like it wet?

do you
want me gone?

do i
see right?
            see?
                    saw?

country
laugh-in time
ache on, & you

            dropping
            your glasses more
            precisely one
            lens fell out

useless
blameless
looking up
to shout

'it's all falling apart'

(get out, get out)

how we do beat
the leaves at
hanging on

ardour's

fire light
lived in from
within

wind
blowing around this
fire, does not burn
higher

heart light's so
withdrawn

we do not warm
our hollow
backt upstate
snow's ground we
walk on

walkt on past
your eyes you
from outside —

outside
fields tonight contract
tomorrow's quarrel
never without its
shadow under
empty moon

call, turn, come back

who'd suspect we'd endure
cold night below zero tracks
to our front, jays at the back

       bits of meat, of
       scrap, love is the
       moonlight only

       breath smoking
       dream out

release this flesh, this
stript meat even
some bird uses, meagre, to
refuel its spin-off
returning
       empty, down

a moonlight, snow make
heartfire impossible, im/
possible from

          outside to in
          dream enter

ember

we see what might be
us in there, our ardour
dying ash
poor ash & us

the poorer

first cause

this morning sun i saw rise
silent over the empty house
my love two lives now
cheerios in hand, smiles

       beatific
         morning
               son

not mythic, just
begotten one

Constellation
                    (Watts, Newark, Detroit ...)

Lady
bug lady
running
up table, sky's
aflame your
children are gone

    homeless, the
    song goes
    home
        does not, we

inhabit sky
one foot
      (herculean
on earth which
tables her, she
nervous shakes
quick wings, wait!

the two parts of
your song,
        Night
coming on

my son with milk
satiate
in temporary arms all
children claim
    fearless for
however long —

This Night
Children Burn

blocks &
blocks changing
rockets
home made bomb bursts
nerve system clusters
light in
/corporate

Lady bug
mother of
flame you
cannot fly

milk & the starry
nipple nebulae we
all desire

connect

us in our rights, to
this once & only home
we go on burning

coming home

if it's to
get lost, lose
way as a wave
breaks

    'goodbye'

i am not speaking of
a path, the 'right'
road, no such
wonderlust

weigh all steps
shift weight
to left or right to

a place where one
steps thru all erratic
wanderings down to
touch:

i am here, feel
my weight on the wet
ground

A number of these poems first appeared in the following little magazines: *Athanor, Odda Tala, Origin, Tuatara, Vigilante,* & *Open Letter.* Some of this work was also included in *The Gist of Origin* anthology.

an earlier version of the 'Columbus Poems' appeared in *Imago 16.*

'Mokelumne Hill' was included in *The Story So Far 1.*

sections of 'Rings' first appeared in *Iron, Caterpillar, Io,* & *Tuatara.*

the first edition of *Rings* was published by the Vancouver Community Press as Georgia Straight Writing Supplement: Vancouver Series No. 3.

Cover drawing and end-papers by Kit Marlatt. Back cover photo by D. Alexander. Photos pages 77 & 129 by Bob Watt.

a Canada Council Arts Grant, 1978-79, gave me time to edit & revise what follows.

Thanks to bpNichol, Nelson Adams, Sarah Sheard & Michael Ondaatje for editorial comments, valuable criticism and technical help.

previous books:

Frames: of a Story. Toronto: Ryerson Press, 1968.
leaf leaf/s. Los Angeles: Black Sparrow Press, 1969.
Rings. Vancouver: Vancouver Community Press, 1971.
Vancouver Poems. Toronto: Coach House Press, 1972.
Steveston, with photographs by Robert Minden. Vancouver: Talonbooks, 1974. Text now available in *The Long Poem Anthology,* edited by Michael Ondaatje, Coach House Press.
Our Lives. Carrboro, North Carolina: Truck Press, 1975.
Zócalo. Toronto: Coach House Press, 1977.
The Story, She Said. Vancouver: B.C. Monthly Press, 1977.
'In the Month of Hungry Ghosts,' *The Capilano Review* 16/17, spring 1979.
Net Work: Selected Writing, edited by Fred Wah. Vancouver: Talonbooks, 1980.
Our Lives. Oolichan Press, 1980.

also edited:

Steveston Recollected: A Japanese-Canadian History. Victoria: B.C. Provincial Archives, 1975.
Opening Doors: Vancouver's East End, with Carole Itter. Victoria: B.C. Provincial Archives, 1979.

Seen through the Press by bpNichol.

Typeset in Aldus and printed in Canada
in an edition of 750 copies, at
THE COACH HOUSE PRESS,
401 (rear) Huron Street,
Toronto, Canada M5S 2G5